WEREWOLVES

WEREWOLVES

by DANIEL COHEN

COBBLEHILL BOOKS

DUTTON   NEW YORK

Library of Congress Cataloging-in-Publication Data
Cohen, Daniel, date
Werewolves / by Daniel Cohen.
p.   cm.
Includes bibliographical references.
Summary: Surveys the world of werewolves, from ancient times to
the Internet.
ISBN 0-525-65207-8
1. Werewolves—Juvenile literature.   [1. Werewolves.]   I. Title.
GR830.W4C65   1996
398'.469—dc20   95-34934   CIP   AC

Published in the United States by Cobblehill Books,
an affiliate of Dutton Children's Books,
a division of Penguin Books USA Inc.,
375 Hudson Street, New York, New York 10014

Designed by Mina Greenstein
Printed in the United States of America
First Edition   10 9 8 7 6 5 4 3 2 1

FOR LON CHANEY, JR.

CONTENTS

WEREWOLVES

INTRODUCTION

Pity the Werewolf

➤ Among monsters in modern times the werewolf has become something of a poor relation. Most of our perceptions about what the great monsters look and act like were formed by a series of motion pictures made by Hollywood's Universal Studios in the 1930s and '40s. The first of these films was *Dracula*, which not only popularized the vampire, but gave its star, Bela Lugosi, a sort of immortality. Then there was *Frankenstein*, which made an instantly recognizable international celebrity out of the actor Boris Karloff, who played the monster. The third great film in this monster cycle was *The Wolf Man*, and it is easily as good as the other two. But do you know the name of the actor who played Lawrence Talbot, the tormented werewolf? Probably not. It was Lon Chaney, Jr., and he had half a dozen outings as the werewolf, but he never became nearly as famous as Lugosi or Karloff.

Can you think of the name of any actor who played a werewolf? All right, Jack Nicholson, but that was for *Wolf*, a movie released in 1994, and Nicholson was a big star before he made the film.

Can you think of any famous werewolf books? Plenty of werewolf books have been written, but none are as famous today as *Frankenstein*, *Dracula*, or the modern *Interview with the Vampire*.

Yet this second-class status is quite unfair. Of all the world's monsters, the werewolf is the one that has been most widely believed in, and most widely feared. Yes, people believed in vampires, and from time to time, graves were dug up and corpses mutilated in the hope that this would stop vampire attacks. But it was far more common for living people to be tried and executed for being werewolves.

And talk about fame—Vlad Tepes, the historical model for Dracula, was well known enough in his own day, but as the violent and cruel ruler of a small central European principality. He was not known as a vampire until much later when Bram Stoker, an English writer of fiction, used him as a model for his imaginary vampire. But on March 31, 1590, a man named Peter Stump (or Stumpe, Stumpf, Stube, Stubbe, Stub, etc., since sixteenth-century writers were rather casual about spelling) was executed near the German city of Cologne for being a werewolf. It was a big story. A sensationalized pamphlet giving the details of Stump's horrid crimes as a werewolf, committed over a period of twenty-five years, and his capture, torture, and execution, illustrated with really gruesome drawings, was translated into many languages and was a best-seller throughout Europe. And this was not supposed to be a work of fiction.

Of course there were fictional werewolves as well. From November, 1846, through July, 1847, readers in Britain were enthralled by weekly installments of the adventures of *Wagner the Wehr-Wolf*. It is the first important use of the werewolf theme in English literature. This mid-Victorian thriller, filled with bloody deeds and supernatural horrors, was one of the most popular examples of that species of literature known as "bloods" or "penny dreadfuls." They were called "bloods" for obvious reasons and "penny dreadfuls" because the installments sold for a penny each. The "penny dreadfuls" were not highly regarded by educated people who read "real" novels, but among ordinary folk they were as popular then as the afternoon "soaps" are today.

The creator of *Wagner the Wehr-Wolf* was G.W.M.

Reynolds, one of the most prolific creators of "penny dreadfuls" and one of the most active social reformers of his time. The series concerns the life of Fernand Wagner, who has made a pact with the devil. He is to receive wealth and youth, but at the price of turning into a ravening werewolf once a month.

Here, in Reynolds' own lush prose, is what the transformation was like: "But lo! what awful change is taking place in the form of that doomed being? His handsome countenance elongates into one of savage and brutelike shape;—the rich garment which he wears becomes a rough, shaggy and wiry skin;—his body loses its human contours—his arms and limbs take another form; and, with a frantic howl of misery, to which the woods give horribly faithful reverberations, and with a rush like a hurtling wind the wretch starts wildly away—no longer a man, but a monstrous wolf! . . .

"A little child is in his path—a sweet, blooming, ruddy, noble boy, with violet-colored eyes and flaxen hair,—disporting merrily at a short distance from his parents who are seated at the threshold of their dwelling.

"Suddenly a strange and ominous rush—an unknown trampling of rapid feet falls upon their ears: then the savage cry, a monster sweeps past.

" 'My child! my child!' screams the affrighted mother; and simultaneously the shrill cry of an infant in the sudden agony of death carries desolation to the ear . . ."

Ah! They don't write 'em like that anymore! And that's probably a good thing, too. But this is the sort of stuff that provided the thrills and chills to British laborers and shopgirls a century and a half ago. In the end, Reynolds' work and that of the other "penny dreadful" writers isn't that far removed in spirit and tone from the works of Stephen King and Anne Rice, who provide today's supernatural thrills and chills for the millions.

By the mid-nineteenth century when *Wagner the Wehr-Wolf* was written, educated people no longer seriously believed in werewolves. But a few centuries earlier, when people were still being burned at the stake for being werewolves, churchmen, who were the only large class of educated people, spent a great deal of time grappling with the problems of being a werewolf.

Could a person actually change to another species—into a wolf? Most churchmen assumed that the werewolf was a creature of the devil. But the change from human to wolf and back again was a genuine miracle, and that could be produced only by God. Would God create such a monster?

According to popular belief, a person could become a werewolf after being given a magic ointment or salve, or a garment made of wolfskin which possessed magical properties. Persons accused of being werewolves often confessed to possessing such ointment or garment. The business about becoming a werewolf after being bitten by another werewolf is basically a creation of the movies. "Real" werewolves didn't just bite people, they tore their victims to pieces and ate them.

The educated churchman did not believe, indeed could not believe, that any diabolical entity could command the power to change man into beast. They had a number of other ways of explaining the existence of werewolves. They often said that the devil created the "illusion" of transformation; he made people "think" that they had turned into wolves, and made the victims "think" that they were being attacked by the creature. Another possible explanation was that the spirit of an evil person, or a demon, might take over the body of a real wolf and thus change it into the far more dangerous werewolf. It was possible, therefore, for an evil person to be asleep in his bed at night, or even locked in a cell under the eyes of his jailers, and yet his spirit could roam free as a werewolf. As a result, a lot of people were convicted of being werewolves even after it was proved that they were nowhere near the place where the werewolf had allegedly committed its crimes. Once the charge was made, it was very hard for a person to prove he was not a werewolf.

A third explanation was that the devil could produce only a partial transformation; therefore, the
werewolf never looked exactly like a "real" wolf. It
might have a short tail, or no tail at all; it might walk
on its hind legs, or be a creature with a human body
but the head of a wolf.

All of this discussion could become pretty techni-
cal and obscure, and the theological wrangling was
of little interest to ordinary folk who were afraid of
being eaten. They simply assumed that there were
people who could be physically changed into wolves
in a variety of ways. The werewolves, however, were
creatures of exceptional strength and ferocity and
even more dangerous than "real" wolves.

Now we must stop for a moment and defend the
wolf. One does not have to spend much time study-
ing the history of the werewolf to realize that people
feared not only werewolves, but ordinary wolves as
well.

Here is how one student of werewolf lore de-
scribes the wolf: "The distinctive features of the wolf
are unbridled cruelty, bestial ferocity, and ravening
hunger. His strength, his cunning, his speed were regarded as abnormal, almost eerie qualities; he had
something of the demon, of hell. He is the symbol of
Night and Winter, of Stress and Storm, the dark and
mysterious harbinger of Death."

This is, of course, all nonsense. The wolf is a

predator, and kills other animals for its food, but it is not abnormally cruel, ferocious, or hungry. Wolves kill only what they need to survive; they are intelligent animals that live in well-ordered packs and can be quite affectionate with one another,

Wolves do not normally attack human beings, and never did, except when no other food was available, and often not even then. They would compete with pastoral people, those who raised sheep, goats, and cattle for food, But the wolf that killed a sheep to bring home to feed its family was no crueler or more ferocious than the shepherd who killed a sheep to feed his family. It certainly didn't make any difference to the sheep, who was going to be eaten one way or the other.

For a long time the wolves could compete fairly successfully with the shepherds. But for the last few hundred years people with their guns, and traps, and poisons have had wolves on the run. Far from being a danger in the modern world, wolves have been completely eliminated from most of the areas where they once roamed. Today, people must go to great lengths just to keep the wolf from becoming extinct. We also now know a great deal more about how wolves live in the wild.

Yet the ancient beliefs about "unbridled cruelty" and "bestial ferocity" hang on. Even very modest plans to reintroduce the wolf in tiny portions of its former range in the western United States have brought forth howls — not from the wolves, but howls of protest from ranchers who seem to think that a few wolves will decimate their livestock. The fears are so wildly out of proportion to any real danger wolves might pose that modern ranchers sound a lot like medieval peasants who thought that there was a werewolf in the neighborhood.

In Biblical times, the Hebrews depended primarily on their flocks and herds of livestock. Wolves would have been a danger to them, and so wolves are often portrayed as symbols of evil in the Bible. In much of Europe the wolf was the largest predator people were likely to encounter. So the evil and dangerous reputation continued. As a result, if someone in Christian Europe was going to be transformed into something large, dangerous, and essentially evil, the wolf would be the most likely candidate.

Turning from human to animal is a common belief throughout the world. Outside of Europe, other *were* or man animals figure prominently. In Russia, for example, there are plenty of wolves, and many werewolf stories. But there were also many large bears in Russia, so there are tales of werebears. There are no wolves in Scotland, but there were fierce Scottish wild cats, and so there are Scottish legends of werecats. Among the Eskimos and other peoples of the North there are stories of people being transformed into seals. In Japan there are werefoxes. In Africa there are wereleopards, werehyenas, even stories of a werehippopotamus, if you can imagine. So while the werewolf may be the most common, and certainly the best known of the were animals, it is by no means the only one.

The belief in werewolves has been the subject of a great deal of study. Doctors and psychiatrists have come up with a number of diseases and conditions that appear to explain parts of the belief that a person can be transformed into a wolf. There is, for example, a serious but fortunately extremely rare genetic disease called *porphyria*. It causes a victim to become sensitive to light, therefore making him more likely to go out only at night. Wolves are supposed to go out at night. The disease creates terrible wounds on the skin. One mark of a werewolf was supposed to be wounds and scars caused by running through the forest in wolf form. In porphyria, even the teeth may become red. Certainly, "bloody teeth" would be another mark of a werewolf. Finally, the disease affects the mind. In a primitive community someone suffering from this disease might easily be suspected of being a werewolf by his neighbors.

There is an even rarer condition called *hypertrichosis*, which causes the entire body, including the face, to be covered with a thick coating of body hair.

Those afflicted with this condition look as if they are made up for a part in one of the wolf man movies. The gene which causes the condition has been called "the werewolf gene."

There are also a number of substances made from plants like belladonna, which were used by physicians of an earlier time to treat a variety of diseases. But when taken in large quantities, or rubbed on the skin in a salve, belladonna can produce hallucinations, can make a person believe he has been flying through the air, or has turned into a wolf. There are also certain types of fungus—ergot is the most common—which infect grain and when the grain is eaten, it can create powerful and long-lasting hallucinations. In 1951, nearly 135 people had to be hospitalized and six died from ergot poisoning in the French town of Pont St. Esprit after eating bread made from fungus-infected rye. The victims had horrible visions of being attacked by tigers and snakes and of turning into wild animals. Incidents like this would have been far more common in medieval times when infected grain would have been more common.

These are some of the medical and scientific explanations that have been offered to explain the widespread belief in werewolves. And they probably do explain certain individual werewolf cases. But they could have only supported and confirmed the deep and ancient belief that under certain conditions, and at certain times, a human being can change into a bloodthirsty monster called a werewolf.

But such beliefs are all part of the past. Nobody believes in werewolves today. Right? Wrong! In 1988 the Fox Broadcasting Company began what they called the Werewolf Hotline. During a six-week period the Hotline received more than 340,000 calls from viewers reporting sightings of werewolves and blaming the creatures for a host of unsolved murders. There were even a few calls from people who said that they were werewolves.

So if you think you're a werewolf, or if you think you've seen a werewolf, and even if you don't believe in them but are just interested in werewolves, in the pages that follow you will find a host of werewolf accounts and stories from ancient to modern times. They all go to show that the werewolf is a lot more than a second-rank movie monster.

1

The
Ancient Werewolf

➤ Another name for a werewolf is a *lycanthrope*.
The condition of being a werewolf, or believing that you are a werewolf, is *lycanthropy*. The word
comes from the name Lycaon, a very ancient and
probably mythological Greek king. There are many
stories about Lycaon, most of them quite gruesome,
for he was known as a cruel tyrant. The most famous
of these stories was told by the Roman poet Ovid in
his work, *The Metamorphoses*, which is all about people changing or being changed into a variety of
things, from rocks to animals.

One day, according to Ovid, the great god

Jupiter came to earth because he had heard "scandalous rumors" about the goings-on in Lycaon's kingdom. The god found that "even the scandalous rumors were less than the truth." So Jupiter revealed himself as a god, and the people began to do him homage.

"Lycaon, however, first laughed at their pious prayers, and then exclaimed: 'I shall find out, by an infallible test, whether he be god or mortal: there will be no doubt about the truth.'"

The tyrant's test was that he killed a man, "a hostage sent him by the Molossian people, slit the man's throat with his sharp blade, and cooked his limbs, still warm with life, boiling some and roasting others over the fire. Then he set this banquet on the table." The guest of honor at this cannibal feast was to be Jupiter himself.

Cannibalism was considered a great sin, and the assumption was that if Jupiter could not recognize human flesh, then he was not a god. Unfortunately for Lycaon, Jupiter *was* a god, and he knew immediately what sort of meal had been set before him.

The gods of the Greeks and Romans did not have forgiving natures. Jupiter told his fellow gods, "I with my avenging flames brought the house crashing down upon its household gods, gods worthy of such a master. Lycaon fled, terrified until he reached the safety of the silent countryside. There he uttered howling noises, and his attempts to speak were all in vain. His clothes changed into bristling hairs, his arms and legs, and he became a wolf. His own savage nature showed in his rabid jaws, and he now directed against the flocks his innate lust for killing. He had a mania, even yet, for shedding blood. But, though he was a wolf, he retained some traces of his original shape. The greyness of his hair was the same, his face showed the same violence, his eyes gleamed as before, and he presented the same picture of ferocity."

The evil Lycaon had become the first famous werewolf, and his name became synonymous with the human wolf.

The story of Lycaon has been told in many different and often contradictory forms, and the origins of the tale are entirely lost. According to one popular theory, there once was a savage cult in the area supposedly ruled by Lycaon. This cult engaged in human sacrifice and cannibalism. The wolf was one of the symbols of this cult, and people believed that cult members were sometimes transformed into wolves. But this is all speculation. No one really knows whether this theoretical bloodthirsty wolf cult ever really existed.

Another rich source of werewolf or shapeshifter lore comes from the Scandinavian countries. The idea that a person could change into a wolf or other animal form through the use of magic is one that is found in almost all cultures. Most commonly it was believed that if a person put on an animal skin, or an animal costume, that person would magically inherit some of the qualities of that animal. This is a belief known as "sympathetic magic"—simply put, it is the belief that if you look like something, in a sense you become that thing.

Many peoples, from Native Americans to the people of Central Africa, have practiced this kind of magic in one form or another. But nowhere did the belief take a stranger and more violent form than among the Norsemen, the people who are often known as the Vikings. In old tales of the Norsemen there are warriors called *berserkers*. The term may mean "men in bearskin coats." The Norse were fierce fighters, and none fiercer than the *berserkers*. In battle they would go into a frenzy, they feared nothing, they felt no pain, fought with superhuman strength, and had to be killed, because they would never surrender. We still use the word "beserk" to describe what happens when a person seems to "go crazy" and becomes completely out of control.

Before a battle, the *berserker* would put on a shirt made of bearskin, or wolfskin. (The old sagas use another word, *ulfheobar*, for men in wolf shirts, but today *berserker* is used to describe both types.) Thus clad, the *berserker* would take on all the ferocity of the wild animal. In reality, neither bears nor wolves are that ferocious. They will fight to the death only when trapped and have no alternative. When faced with a stronger foe, most animals, including bears and wolves, will run away. But people believed the animals were that fierce, and it was the belief, not the reality that counted. In a poem written about A.D. 900, it says of a battle: "the berserks bayed . . . the wolf-coats howled." In some of the early Scandinavian art there are battle scenes in which figures of what seem to be bears or wolves with human legs and feet are shown.

In the tenth century, when the Norse were fighting the forces of the Byzantine emperor, one of the churchmen in the emperor's service noted with disapproval that the Norse didn't fight like they did. The Byzantine soldiers, he said, relied on the arts of war. The Norse, he claimed, seemed to be driven by ferocity and blind madness, and fought like wild beasts, "howling in a strange and disagreeable manner."

If going into battle wearing a bearskin or wolfskin could transport a warrior into an almost inhuman fighting frenzy, then it was only a short mental step into believing that a garment made from the skin of an animal could actually turn an individual into that animal.

Scandinavian lore is rich with werewolf tales and in most of these cases the transformation is accomplished by putting on something made of wolfskin. Generally, it was assumed that the werewolf could change back to his human form after a certain period of time, so long as he abstained from eating human flesh while he was a wolf.

2

The Werewolf Trials

During the sixteenth century, France was afflicted with an epidemic of werewolves. Or at least that is what one might believe after examining the records of trials held all over the country. Of course, it is important to know that during this period France, and indeed all of Europe, was caught up in the witch-hunting craze. No one knows how many people were executed in the belief that they were witches. At the time, being a werewolf was regarded as just another form of witchcraft, though a particularly horrible one.

Here are some of the better-known cases.

➔ In December, 1521, two men were being tried after being accused of witchcraft and murder. Their names were Pierre Bourgot, or Peter the Great as people had nicknamed him because of his large size, and Michel Verdung.

The trial had not been going on for long when Peter suddenly burst forth with the amazing confession that he was a werewolf. He said that about nineteen years earlier there had been a great storm which had scattered his flock of sheep. He tried to find the sheep, but without any success.

"Then there rode up three men on black horses, and the last said to me: 'What are you doing? You seem to be in trouble.'"

Peter told him about his lost sheep and the horseman said to cheer up, and promised that his master would protect him. The horseman then told Peter where he could find his missing sheep. And he promised to provide the peasant with money. They agreed to meet a few days later. Following the horseman's instructions, Peter was able to locate his missing flock.

When Peter met the horseman again, he learned that "the master" of which he spoke was the devil. Peter renounced his religion, and kissed the horseman's left hand "which was ice-cold as that of a corpse." He then fell on his knees and gave his allegiance to Satan. At first, Peter's only duties as a servant of the devil appear to have been failing to go to church.

About two years passed. "All anxiety about my flock was removed, for the devil had undertaken to protect it and to keep off the wolves.

"This freedom from care, however, made me begin to tire of the devil's service, and I began to go to church again, until I was brought back into obedience to the evil one by Michel Verdung, when I renewed my compact on the understanding that I should be supplied with money."

At this point things began to get really serious. Peter attended a gathering of witches in a wood near Chastel Charnon. He smeared his body with some sort of salve or ointment given to him by Michel Verdung, and "I believed myself then to be transformed into a wolf. I was at first horrified at my wolf's feet, and the fur with which I was covered all at once, but I found that I could now travel with the speed of the wind. This could not have taken place without the help of our powerful master, who was present during our excursion, though I did not perceive him until I had resumed my human form. Michel did the same as myself.

"When we had been transformed for one or two hours, Michel smeared us again, and quick as thought we resumed our human forms. The salve was given to us by our masters."

After this first transformation, the murders began. Pierre said that at one point, while in his wolf form, he attacked a boy of about six or seven with his teeth, but the boy screamed so loudly that he was forced to retreat, and to smear himself with the ointment and change back to human form to escape detection.

The boy was extremely lucky, for in later attacks Pierre and Michel killed several children.

The record concludes: "The statements of Pierre Bourgot were fully corroborated by Michel Verdung." There is no indication of what happened to the two self-confessed werewolves, but it is highly unlikely that they survived for long after their confession.

➤ In late autumn of 1573, the following pronouncement was read out in the public square of villages around the city of Dole, in the area known as Franche Comte:

"According to the advertisement made to the sovereign Court of Parliament at Dole, that, in the territories of Espagny, Salvange, Courchapon, and the neighboring villages, has often been seen and met, for some time past, a werewolf, who, it is said, has already seized and carried off several little children, so that they have not been seen since, and since he has attacked and done injury in the country to some horsemen, who kept him off only with great difficulty and danger to their persons; the said Court, desiring to prevent any greater danger, has permitted, and does permit, those who are abiding or dwelling in the said places and others, notwithstanding all edicts concerning the chase, to assemble with pikes, halberts, arquebuses, and sticks to chase and to pursue the said werewolf in every place where they may find or seize him; to tie and kill, without incurring any pains or penalties . . . Given at the meeting of the said Court, on the thirteenth day of the month September 1573."

This call to gather with pikes, sticks, and all other available weapons in order to "chase and to pursue the said werewolf" conjures up images from all of those old horror films where the peasants gather with pitchforks and lighted torches to pursue the monster. The difference is that this is not a scene from a movie, it really happened.

On November 8, 1573, some peasants returning home from work through the forest heard the screams of a child, and the deep baying of a wolf. They ran in the direction of the sounds and found a horrible sight. A little girl was defending herself against a monstrous creature that had already wounded her severely. As the peasants approached, the creature fled on all fours into the forest. It was nearly dark when this took place, so that the creature could not be identified with certainty. Some said it was a wolf, while others insisted it was a man, moreover a man they knew—Gilles Garnier.

Garnier was just the sort of man whom one might expect would be accused of being a werewolf. He lived with his wife in an isolated hovel nearby. Garnier was an ugly man with a pronounced stoop, a livid complexion, and deep-set eyes under a pair of coarse and bushy brows, which met in the middle of his forehead. Eyebrows that met in the middle of the forehead were often considered one sign of a werewolf. Garnier lived such an isolated life that people called him "the Hermit of St. Bonnot."

On November 14, a ten-year-old boy disappeared somewhere in the vicinity of Garnier's hovel, and at that point "the Hermit of St. Bonnot" was seized and brought to trial. Under torture, he quickly confessed to a whole series of murders while he was in the form of a wolf. He was executed within a few days.

→ An example of an entire family accused of being werewolves comes from the writing of Henri Boguet, Chief Justice of Saint-Claude in the late sixteenth century. He presided at many witchcraft and werewolf trials.

In 1598, Pernette Gandillon, who had a habit of running around the countryside on all fours believing she was a wolf, attacked two small children. The boy tried to fight her off with a knife, but she took it away from him and stabbed him. Almost immediately she was killed by an angry mob.

The day after Pernette was killed, her brother Pierre and his son Georges were accused of witchcraft. Both also confessed to being werewolves. Pierre said that he turned into a wolf after rubbing his body with a magic salve. He said he was able to return to human form by rolling in the wet grass.

In *The Book of Werewolves*, author Sabine Baring-Gould writes, "Pierre and Georges in prison behaved as maniacs, running on all fours about their cells and howling dismally. Their faces, arms, and legs were frightfully scarred with the wounds they had received from dogs when they had been on their raids. Bourget accounts for the transformation not taking place by the fact of their not having the necessary salves by them."

Pierre, Georges, and another sister, Antoinette, who confessed only to being a witch, were all executed.

➤ On December 14, 1598, a tailor from Paris was sentenced to death for being a werewolf. When his house was searched, a whole barrel full of human bones was found. The details of the trial were so horrible that after it was over the judges ordered that all the documents relating to the case be destroyed.

➤ These are just a few samples of the many, many trials of accused werewolves that took place in sixteenth-century France. Gruesome and horrible as they are, cases of murder and mutilation can be found throughout history—even in America today. The difference is that today we do not believe that people who commit such crimes have been transformed into wolves. But in sixteenth-century France, in the middle of the witch hunts, many people believed that such a transformation was not only possible, but common. That is what makes the story of Jean Grenier so unusual.

During the early spring of 1603, there was a virtual reign of terror in the St. Sever district of Gascony in the extreme southwest of France. Children began to disappear and no trace of them could be found. Once an infant was actually taken out of its crib where its mother had left it for just a few moments. People talked of wolves; others shook their heads and whispered of something worse than wolves.

Then some witnesses came forward with strange stories. A thirteen-year-old girl named Marguerite Poirier, of the hamlet of St. Paul, said that one afternoon, while she was tending the cattle, she was attacked by a ferocious doglike animal with reddish fur and a short, stumpy tail. It had torn at her skirt with its claws. She managed to save herself by hitting the creature with an iron-tipped staff that she carried.

Later, others in the area reported that a boy of about fourteen, named Jean Grenier, boasted that it was he who had attacked Marguerite while in the form of a wolf. He said that if it had not been for the stick, he would have killed and eaten her, as he had already done to others.

An eighteen-year-old named Jeanne Gaboriaut told a court under oath that both she and Jean Grenier were servants of a well-to-do farmer, and that they tended cattle together. According to the girl, Grenier said that he had a wolf's pelt that had been given to him by a man named Pierre Labourat, and when he put it on he was able to turn into a wolf. He also said, as had many others accused of being werewolves, that he had a magic salve, which helped the transformation from human to wolf and back again.

Jean Grenier was arrested and brought before

the court. He was the son of a poor laborer. For the last several months he had been wandering about the countryside, working for different farmers and watching their flocks. But he was usually discharged because he neglected his duties. When not working, he tried to support himself by begging. When asked if he was a werewolf, he freely admitted that he was, and that he had already killed and eaten several children, and tried to attack many others. Grenier described how he had attacked a little boy whom he would have killed if a man had not come to the rescue. As he fled, Grenier shouted, "I'll have you yet." The man who saved the child came forward and corroborated Grenier's statement, including the final shout, "I'll have you yet."

More witnesses came forward to say that they had seen the boy in the area when some of the crimes had been committed. The case against Jean Grenier seemed overwhelming, and if it had followed the course of most of the werewolf trials in France, he would have been condemned to death by burning. But the chief of the court made an eloquent speech. He said that he would put aside all the questions of witchcraft and pacts with the devil and transformation into a wolf. He stated courageously that the court should only consider the boy's age and the fact that he was so dull and idiotic that he had the mind of a much younger child. The chief of the court went on to observe that the transformation into a wolf was something that took place only within Jean Grenier's disordered brain.

In the end, the court sentenced Grenier to perpetual imprisonment within the walls of a monastery at Bordeaux, but if he attempted to escape he would immediately be put to death.

This case is unusual in another respect; it contains a follow-up report. Some seven years after he was confined to the monastery, Jean Grenier was described as being very small in stature and, far from being a fierce werewolf, he was so shy that he could not look anyone in the face. His eyes were deep-set and restless, his teeth long and protruding, and his nails black and worn away. His mental condition had deteriorated further, and he seemed unable to understand even the simplest question.

He died in the monastery at the age of twenty.

→ Jean Grenier was not the first individual accused of being a werewolf who was found to be mad. In 1598, Jacques Rollet of the parish of Maumusson near Nantes was accused of killing a boy. The boy's mangled body was found by some villagers. As they approached the body, three wolves bounded into the forest. While tracking the wolves, the villagers found Rollet, his beard and hands covered with blood, cowering in the forest.

He was brought before a judge and quickly confessed to having been one of the three wolves. The other wolves, he said, were his companions, Jean and Julian. In addition to killing the boy, Rollet also confessed to killing and eating women, lawyers, attorneys, and bailiffs, though he said that the bailiffs were tough and tasteless.

Rollet was first condemned to death, but later was found to be so confused and pathetic that he was finally sent to a madhouse. But it was the Grenier case that marked the real change. After that, there was a growing belief that people who thought that they were werewolves were insane.

➤ Though the trial and execution of individuals accused of being werewolves had practically died out by the seventeenth century, belief in the reality of the werewolf hung on in many parts of Europe.

In 1685, the Bavarian town of Ansbach was afflicted by what appeared to be a large and particularly vicious wolf. The creature killed several women and children and a large number of cattle.

The rumor spread that the creature was not a natural wolf, but a werewolf, though a werewolf of an unusual sort. It was supposed to be the spirit or ghost of a recently dead burgomaster or mayor, a man of evil reputation. When a large wolf was finally caught and killed, its carcass was dressed in the burgomaster's clothes. A chestnut-colored wig was placed on its head, and after the animal's snout was cut off, a mask resembling the dead burgomaster was put on its face.

This grotesque creation was first hung in the town square, and then stuffed and put on display in a museum. It was pointed to as proof of the existence of actual werewolves.

3

The Beast of Le Gevaduan

For three years, beginning in the year 1764, the region of France known as Le Gevaduan was terrorized by a monster wolf. Of all of history's werewolf accounts, this tale of what is commonly called "the Beast of Le Gevaduan" is the best documented, the most puzzling, and in its way, the most frightening.

Le Gevaduan is a rugged, mountainous region. The land is too rocky for farming and most of the people survived by tending flocks of sheep and herds of cattle.

During the summer months the animals grazed in

high and often isolated mountain pastures. Children were traditionally sent to watch over the sheep and cattle. In mid-July, 1764, a young girl from the village of Saint Etienne de Lugdares, who had been tending a flock of sheep, failed to return home as expected. Later, her body was found in one of the valleys. Her heart had been torn out. This was the first recorded killing in the reign of the Beast, but it was by no means the last. In the following days the killings of several other children who had been watching over flocks in isolated areas were reported.

As word of the killings spread, there was a panic among the peasants of the region. Frightened parents kept their children at home, for a while. But time passed. There were no more killings reported. The livestock could not go unattended forever. The old ways of sending the children out to guard the livestock reasserted themselves.

Then, late in August, a peasant woman from the village of Langogne told her neighbors that she had seen a fantastic creature. It walked on two legs like a man, but it was covered with short reddish hair and had a piglike snout. It was as big as a donkey and had rather short ears and a long tail. The woman said the creature had been able to frighten off her dogs, but had been frightened itself by her cattle, which lowered their heads and attacked it with their horns.

This witness was not considered particularly

trustworthy, and the description itself was so bizarre that even the most superstitious peasants just laughed at it at first. The laughing stopped a few days later, however, when the monster was reported again. This time the witness was Jean-Pierre Pourcher, a man known for his truthfulness and for his courage. Jean-Pierre got close enough to the monster to actually take a shot at it with his musket. He was a good marksman, but this time the shot either missed or the creature was unaffected by the bullet. It ran away swiftly.

And the murders of children began again. Some of those who had been allowed to return to the flocks in isolated pastures fell victim to a creature that not only killed, but mutilated, its victims. It was then that the rumors began to circulate that the region was afflicted by a *loup-garou*, as the werewolf is called in France.

News of the murders eventually reached the court of King Louis XV at Versailles. The king took the matter very seriously, for as we have seen, stories of werewolves were numerous in France. The king dispatched a company of soldiers to deal with the Beast. The soldiers arrived in February, 1765, and almost immediately encountered the creature, or what they believed to be the creature. They opened fire on it, but it ran off into the underbrush and could not be located. After the encounter, the killings appeared to stop. The soldiers assumed that they mortally wounded the Beast and that it had crawled off to some hidden place and died. They returned to the palace at Versailles to report that their mission had been successfully accomplished. The report was premature.

As the weather warmed up, the children once again returned to the mountain valleys to tend the sheep and cattle. And there were more killings. Another urgent appeal was sent to the king at Versailles, but the king was slow to respond. It wasn't until early in 1766 that another military expedition was sent to the area.

This time the soldiers were able to shoot a large wolf, which they confidently declared to be "the Beast of Le Gevaduan." They marched back to Versailles in triumph. The king heard their report and once again declared the emergency to be over. And once again he was wrong.

The thing, whatever it was, continued to stalk Le Gevaduan. Several villages were actually abandoned out of fear of the monster. Finally, in June, 1767, nearly three years after the killings began, a local nobleman organized a huge party of hunters. He swore that they would not rest until the monster really and finally had been killed.

On June 19, what the hunters believed to be the Beast was surrounded in a patch of woods at Le

Sogne d'Auvert. One of the hunters, a man named Jean Chastel, had his gun loaded with silver bullets. There is a well-known tradition that only a silver bullet can kill a werewolf. When he caught sight of the Beast, Chastel was able to fire two shots at it. The second struck the monster in the heart and it fell dead.

The carcass was then carried from village to village as proof that the terrible Beast of Le Gevaduan was finally, really and truly, dead. Unfortunately, the accounts of exactly what the thing looked like are not as clear as one would wish. Most descriptions make it sound like a very large but strange-looking wolf, with close-croped ears and unusual hooflike feet.

In the warm June weather, the carcass soon began to rot and had to be buried. While no one seems to know where the monster was buried, tourists are still shown the spot where Jean Chastel is supposed to have felled it with a silver bullet. Chastel's gun can be seen in the church at Saint Martin-de-Bouchaux.

What was the Beast of Le Gevaduan? Clearly it was more than just a legend. The records that indicate that something deadly and dangerous was stalking the area in the 1760s are too numerous and too reliable to be ignored. Some people believe that the Beast was just a large and exceptionally ferocious wolf, or perhaps several wolves whose killings were attributed to a single creature by the terrified peasants. The peasants may also have exaggerated the number and nature of the killings, attributing unrelated deaths to the Beast.

One theory holds that there was an outbreak of rabies among the wolves of Le Gevaduan and that the disease caused them to behave in such a vicious and uncharacteristic manner. Normally, wolves avoid human beings at all costs. The only time a wolf might be tempted to attack a human would be during times of famine in the winter, when it was starving and no other prey was available. But the attacks of the Beast took place in the warm months when prey for the wolf would have been abundant. Rabies, on the other hand, tends to flourish in the warmer weather.

Others think the Beast was really a man—a homicidal madman who never was caught, but just happened to die at about the same time Chastel shot a large wolf.

And then there are those who believe that the Beast of Le Gevaduan was just exactly what the peasants thought that it was—the *loup-garou*, the werewolf.

In any case, this is among the most interesting and best documented of all werewolf accounts.

4

The Christmas Werewolf

Which holiday do you think would be most closely associated with werewolves?

You would almost certainly guess Halloween, and think of people running around in furry and fanged masks. But your guess would be wrong. There is a holiday associated with werewolves, but it isn't Halloween, it's Christmas, particularly in northern Europe.

Olaus Magnus, a sixteenth-century Swedish churchman and historian, and one of the most learned men of his age, wrote a long account of the traditions and beliefs of the Scandinavian people.

The werewolf is one of the beliefs that comes up most frequently. He wrote:

"On the feast of the nativity of Christ, at night, such a multitude of wolves transformed from men gather together in a certain spot, arranged among themselves, and then spread to rage with wondrous ferocity against human beings, and those animals which are not wild, and the natives of these regions suffer more from these than they do from true and natural wolves. When a human habitation has been detected by the werewolves, they besiege it with ferocity, trying to break in the doors, and if they do so, they devour all the human beings, and every animal found inside. They burst into the beer cellars and there they empty the casks of beer or mead, and pile up the empty cases in the middle of the cellar, thus showing their difference from natural and genuine wolves . . ."

This presents the horrifying spectacle of hordes of drunken werewolves.

Olaus continues: "Between Lithuania, Livonia, and Courland [in the region called the Baltics] are the walls of a certain old ruined castle. At this spot congregate thousands, on a fixed occasion, and try their agility in jumping. Those who are unable to bound over the wall, as is often the case with the fattest, are fallen upon with scourages [whips] by the captains and slain."

➤ In the sixteenth century, another curious Christmas story of the Livonians appeared in the chronicles of the era. It was said that at Christmas a lame boy went around the countryside summoning all the devil's followers, "who are countless," to a general conclave. Anyone who failed to appear or who seemed to go reluctantly was beaten by a man with an iron whip, "till the blood flows, and his traces are left in blood."

Soon the human form of these servants of the devil vanished and they all became wolves, many thousands of them. The leader with the iron whip went first, followed by the troop, "firmly convinced in their imaginations that they are transformed into wolves."

These would-be werewolves would then attack herds of cattle and flocks of sheep, but they apparently lacked the power to kill people "When they come to a river, the leader smites the water with his whip, and it divides, leaving a dry path through the midst, by which the pack may go. The transformation lasts twelve days, at the expiration of which period the wolfskin vanishes, and the human form reappears."

It is not clear whether the churchmen who wrote about these Livonian beliefs thought that the individuals were actually transformed into wolves, or merely believed that they were. But the church was sufficiently concerned about the stories to expressly forbid people to believe them.

➤ Why do werewolf legends so often center around the Christmas season? These legends almost certainly predate Christianity. The Christmas season is also the time of the winter solstice, the darkest and often coldest time of the year. In northern Europe it could be a frightening time, and it would be a time when wolves driven by hunger might represent their greatest threat to humans and their livestock. In the cold and the dark, with wolves howling in the distance, it would be a time that people might think about werewolves. It would also be a time when some people were driven to the edge of madness by the isolation, and by hunger. Such hardships could drive people to think of themselves as wolves. All in all, it is not so surprising that the traditionally joyous celebration of Christmas is also the werewolves' holiday.

While the association of werewolves and Christmas was most common in northern Europe, the best-known Christmas werewolf of all comes from the village of St. Angelo in the Lombardy region of sunny Italy.

Several centuries ago, a boy was born to a couple

in the village on Christmas Eve. It was no happy event, for all the villagers knew what that meant — the boy was destined to become a werewolf.

The village of St. Angelo was a small and close-knit community. The villagers realized that this curse was not the fault of the parents, and certainly no fault of the infant. So they banded together to help the family.

The child was allowed to grow up in peace, just as if he were a normal child. And he displayed an unusually pleasant and gentle nature. He played with the other children of the village and there were never any problems — until Christmas Eve came around.

As the bells tolled for Midnight Mass, the boy was transformed. He tore off his clothes and fell to the ground groaning and foaming at the mouth. He rolled around in the street as his body changed. And when he rose up, he was a wolf which attacked his parents, friends, and neighbors, anyone who was nearby.

While the boy was small, he was transformed into a small wolf. The villagers of St. Angelo were able to restrain him and keep him from doing any harm. As he got older and larger, they were able to fend him off with sticks, though they always took care not to hurt him.

After that, they began locking up their livestock and themselves on Christmas Eve. Prevented from killing anyone or anything in the village, the were-wolf would run off into the woods, and the villagers would spend the night keeping a careful watch and praying for the boy's soul.

On Christmas morning the boy, once again in his human form, would return, filthy and bloodstained from his night of rampaging in the woods. He would be exhausted and sleep most of the day. But when he awoke, all trace of the wild animal had vanished, and he was able to resume his normal life.

Though everyone knew of his affliction, he was still very popular. When he was twenty-three, he married the daughter of a farmer, a girl he had known all his life. They were a happy couple, but a careful one. They planned for Christmas Eve. Well before midnight, the wife would send her husband out of the house. She would not open the door under any circumstances until she heard three loud raps. This was the prearranged signal that the werewolf had resumed his human form and was no longer a danger. She would then carefully wash him and put him to bed.

This arrangement continued successfully for several years—until, on one Christmas Eve the wife apparently became careless. The villagers were only able to guess at what had happened the next morning. They found the husband running through the streets of the village filthy and caked with blood. He was muttering loudly to himself, but no one could make out what he was saying.

The villagers threw a blanket over him and took him back to his home. What they found was a scene of horror. The door to the little house was swinging open. Inside all was in chaos. It seemed as if every piece of crockery in the house had been shattered, every bit of cloth shredded. On the floor in the midst of the chaos lay the body of the young woman. It had been mutilated and chewed almost beyond recognition.

The villagers assumed that the wife had either forgotten to lock the door securely, or had made a mistake and opened the door too soon. They couldn't regard the husband as a murderer, but they were no longer able to view him with the tolerant kindness of earlier years. They withdrew from him.

One night, the husband, unable to live with the knowledge of what he was, and what he had done, stabbed himself to death. The villagers buried him beside his wife. After the ceremony they felt more of a sense of relief than of sadness.

➤ There are quite a number of other stories of werewolves who tried, somehow, to live with their condition. They would prepare a secret room in their house. When the time for the transformation was upon them, and that might be every night, only when there was a full moon, or—like the werewolf of St. Angelo—once a year, they would lock themselves in the room.

Usually these rooms would be in a remote corner of a large house, or insulated in such a way that the howls and growls of the werewolf would not be heard by the neighbors. The rooms would also be fitted out with an elaborate series of locks. The locks could be easily opened by a human being, but could not be handled by a wolf. In that way, the beast would be kept confined until it resumed its human state.

Of course, as we have seen, the precautions didn't always work.

5

Werewolves of the North

From northern Europe come a huge number of tales of werewolves. Here is just a brief selection of some of these accounts. They will give you some idea of just how extensive and varied the werewolf belief was in that part of the world.

From Sweden comes a tale of a soldier from the province of Kalmar who had fought in the war with Russia in 1808–09. He became homesick, and he returned to his native land, but in the shape of a wolf. Unluckily, he was shot by a hunter just outside of the village in which he had lived. When the dead wolf, a huge beast, was skinned, a shirt was discovered in-

side the wolfskin. A woman identified the shirt as
one she had sewn for her soldier husband just before
he left for the war in Russia.

→　　There is an old Norse legend about
Sigmund, the robber, and his son. One summer day
they were in the forest, looking for something to steal
when they came upon a house in which there were
two sleeping men. The two men wore large gold
rings, which were of great interest to the robber and
his son. As it happened, these two men were the sons
of kings, but had become werewolves, or "skin
changers" as they are called in the legend. For nine
days they were wolves. On the tenth day they were
able to take off their wolfskins and become human
for twenty-four hours. Above the two sleeping men
hung two shirts made from wolfskin.

Traditionally, it is believed that after resuming his
human shape the werewolf is completely exhausted
from his exertions as a wild beast, and sleeps deeply.
These two sleepers did not awake when the robber
and his son entered their house. Sigmund and his son
put on the wolf shirts, but were unable to take them
off and soon turned into wolves themselves. They
howled like wolves, but were able to understand one
another perfectly. For nine days they roamed the forest living like wolves. On the tenth day the robber

and his son returned to the house, and were able to take off the wolfskin shirts. They immediately built a fire and burned them.

→   Olaus Magnus had another story about Livonia. He said that the wife of a very important nobleman once said that men could not be turned into wolves. One of her servants asked her permission to give her an example of how men could indeed turn into wolves. She agreed. The servant went into the cellar and a few moments later a large wolf came out. The wolf ran out of the house, but was followed by a pack of dogs. The dogs managed to overtake the wolf and bit out one of its eyes in the fight. The next day the servant came to his lady, but now he had only one eye.

→   From northern Hungary comes this late nineteenth-century account. There was a very poor Gypsy fiddler named Kropan. He was barely able to make enough money to feed himself and his wife. And he had another worry as well. His wife often disappeared at night. He suspected that she was seeing another man, and he tried to watch her secretly. When she thought he was asleep, she got up and slipped out of the hut. At dawn a huge grey wolf carrying a dead lamb in its jaws slipped into the hut. The man fainted, and the next thing he knew his wife was roasting him a dish of lamb.

Kropan said nothing, but from that day forward his wife supplied him with the best meats—sheep, calves, cows, and pigs. There was so much meat that Kropan began selling the surplus in nearby towns. He didn't sell the meat in his own village because he didn't want his neighbors to know what he was doing.

Soon he made so much money selling meat that he was able to buy an inn, which became very popular because the food was so cheap. But after a while suspicions were aroused, particularly since the wolf had done so much damage to the local livestock.

The villagers bound Kropan and his wife, and a priest exorcised them, sprinkling them with holy water. As drops of holy water touched the woman, she reacted as if she had been hit with boiling oil. Then she simply disappeared. The enraged peasants killed Kropan. The records show that two of the peasants who took part in the killing of Kropan were actually imprisoned for six years in the jail of Ilova. They were released in 1881.

→ Among the inhabitants of a certain part of Russia there was a curious belief in a creature called the *wawklak*. This is a man who has been transformed into a wolf by the devil. But this wolf goes among his friends and relatives, who recognize him and feed him well. "He is a most amiably disposed werewolf, for he does no mischief, and testifies his affection for his kindred by licking their hands." The *wawklak*, however, is driven by an irresistible passion for a change of scene. He can't stay in any one place for long, but travels from house to house, from village to village.

➔ A common belief in northern Europe was that a person was transformed into a wolf by putting on a shirt or cloak or belt made of wolfskin. There is the story of a man who had such a belt, but forgot one day when he was going out, to lock up the belt. While he was away his little son found the belt, and buckled it around himself. The boy was instantly turned into an animal that, to all outward appearances, looked more like a bundle of straw and was only able to roll around on the floor. When the neighbors saw what had happened, they immediately searched out the father, who was able to unbuckle the belt before the child did any harm. Later, the boy said that when he put the belt on he was seized with such a raging hunger that he was ready to tear to pieces and devour anything that came his way.

6

The Wound
of the Werewolf

One of the earliest werewolf stories on record
dates back to the days of ancient Rome. It was
written by a man named Petronius, an official of the
court of Emperor Nero, in about A.D. 60. Petronius
wrote of a magnificent banquet given by the newly
wealthy Trimalchio. At the banquet the revelers tell
stories, and this is one told by a former servant
named Niceros.

Niceros said that while he was still a servant, he
was seeing a woman named Melissa Tarentina. One
evening when Melissa was staying with a friend in
the country, Niceros decided to visit her. But it was a

walk of about four or five miles to where Melissa was staying, and Niceros did not wish to make the journey alone, particularly at night.

"I laid hold of the opportunity, and persuaded my friend to take an evening's walk of four or five miles out of town, for he was a stout fellow, and as bold as a devil. The moon shone as bright as day and at one point we passed a cemetery. My friend loitered behind me star-gazing . . ."

Niceros sat down and waited for his friend to catch up. "I was sitting expecting him . . . when looking round me, what should I see but my friend stript stark-naked, and his clothes lying beside the highway."

Then, quite suddenly, the man turned into a wolf. "Don't think I jest, I value no man's estate at that rate, as to tell a lie. But as I was saying, after he was turned into a wolf, he set up a howl, and fled to the woods."

Niceros admitted that at first he did not know what to do. But he boasted, "Another man would have died of fear, but I drew my sword . . ." And thus armed, he made his way to the house where Melissa was staying.

By the time he got to the house, Niceros felt terrible. "I entered the door; my eyes were sunk in my head, the sweat ran off me by more than one stream, and I felt as if I were breathing my last."

Melissa came up to him, but she wasn't very sympathetic: "You should have come sooner, you would have done us a favor. A wolf attacked the farm and has made butchers' work among the cattle. The wolf got away, but he had no reason to laugh, for a servant of ours got him through the neck with a pitchfork."

"As soon as I heard her, I ran home. Passing the place where my friend's clothes had been, I saw nothing but a puddle of blood. When I got home I found my friend lying in bed, with the doctor dressing a large wound in his neck.

"I understood afterwards that he was a fellow who could change his skin. But from that day forward, I could never eat a bite of bread with him, not if you'd have killed me."

➔ Petronius' book in which this tale appeared is a work of fiction, not meant to be taken too seriously. But the tale is clearly rooted in beliefs that are far older than the Roman Empire itself. One of the core elements of Niceros' account is that if you wound a werewolf while in the wolf state, the wound will persist after the transformation. This belief was passed down through the ages, and for centuries could be found in werewolf accounts from many different parts of the world.

Gervase of Tilbury, an English scholar who wrote during the early years of the eleventh century, noted that "In England we often see men changed into wolves at the changes of the moon." Gervase tells the story of one Raimbaud, a former soldier turned outlaw. He was forced to live by his wits in the forest like an animal. As a result, he turned into a werewolf and began to attack both children and adults. It was commonly believed that a person who lived like an animal might become an animal.

Raimbaud's rampages continued until one day the werewolf attacked a carpenter, who happened to have his tools with him. The carpenter was able to chop off one of the wolf's hind paws. Then, according to the story, the wolf immediately reverted to human form and thanked the carpenter for ridding him "forever of the accursed and damned form." As a result of this account, Gervase observed, "It is commonly reported and held by grave and worthy doctors that if a werewolf be shorn of one of his members, he shall surely recover his original body."

➔ In 1588, this story was told in France. In the mountains of Auvergne a nobleman was looking out of the window of his castle and saw a hunter that he knew. He called out to the hunter and told him to report any luck that he had. While in the forest, the hunter was attacked by a large wolf. He fired at the animal with his gun, but the shot missed. Then, just as it sprang at him, he struck at it with his hunting knife, and managed to sever one of the beast's paws. The wounded wolf quickly retreated into the forest. The hunter picked up the paw and put it in his knapsack.

When the hunter reached the castle, he told the nobleman of his close encounter with a wolf, and to emphasize his story he opened his knapsack. But to his horror and surprise, he found not a wolf's paw as he had expected, but the hand of a woman which had a gold ring on one of the fingers.

The nobleman recognized the ring as belonging to his wife. He rushed to her room to question her, and found her with one arm hidden beneath the folds of a shawl. He pulled the shawl aside and saw that she had lost her hand. Then she confessed that it was she who had attacked the hunter while in the form of a wolf. She was arrested and executed shortly afterward at Ryon.

In another story from France, a noblewoman who was a werewolf had her paw mangled in a trap during one of her nightly forays as a wolf. For the rest of her life, she was forced to wear a glove to conceal her deformed hand.

➤ When French settlers came to Canada, they brought the werewolf or, as it was commonly known, *loup-garou* beliefs with them. Here is a story that was told by French Canadians as early as the seventeenth century.

In the village of Saint-Antoine in the district of Beausejour, there was a miller named Joachim Crete. He was a solitary and rather unfriendly man, but he did his work, bothered no one, and he was well enough thought of in the community. His hired man, Hubert Sauvageau, was another matter entirely. He was widely disliked, mainly because he was surly and never attended church.

Joachim, however, didn't care. As far as he was concerned, a man's beliefs were his own. Hubert was a responsible and diligent worker, and the best checkers partner in Beausejour. Most evenings when work was over, Joachim and his hired man would sit down in front of the fire with a bottle of brandy and play checkers until it was time to go to bed. Hubert's only oddity was that occasionally he would disappear in the evening, never saying where he was going. But he was always back and ready for work the next morning. Once again, Joachim's "live and let live" attitude was that so long as the man did his job, it was no business of his what he did with his evenings when he was not working.

On one such evening, Joachim was sitting by the fire when he heard a terrible commotion outside. He rushed out of the door and found a sleigh which had just overturned, spilling a young woman and her three children onto the snow. The horse that pulled the sleigh was panicky and out of control. Joachim was able to quiet the horse, and he took the little family into his house so they could warm up. He asked them what had happened.

"It's the *loup-garou*," the woman said. "It stood in our path and our poor horse was frozen with fear. Then she took off and knocked the wolf aside before it could sink its teeth into her neck."

Joachim tried to reassure the frightened woman. There were wolves in the area, he said, but they were ordinary wolves, and not really dangerous to humans. Oh, yes, he had heard about the *loup-garou* many times, but he did not believe such tales, they were all superstition. But the woman could not be reassured, so he escorted them home.

The miller was not just trying to calm the woman. He really didn't believe in the *loup-garou*, but still he felt a little uneasy while returning home. He didn't feel any better when he found Hubert in the house, looking more unkempt and disreputable than ever and in a deep sleep. It is often said that a werewolf is exhausted after returning to human form, and must sleep for several hours to regain his strength. Joachim tried to tell himself that nothing was wrong, and he was almost able to convince himself of that—almost.

Weeks went by and nothing seemed to happen, and Joachim began to feel he had been foolish in suspecting his hired hand of being a *loup-garou*. Then it was Christmas Eve. The miller and his hired hand were getting ready to spend the evening drinking and playing checkers as they had often done before. Some of Joachim's neighbors stopped by to ask if he was going to attend Midnight Mass. No, the miller said, this was just another night, and Christmas Day was just another working day as far as he was concerned. He even started his millstone turning.

Joachim and Hubert played and drank, and the millstone continued to turn. Both men had drunk more than usual. At the stoke of midnight, the millstone stopped turning. The two men, now quite drunk, rose from the table and went out to set it going again. Nothing appeared to be broken, but still they couldn't get it started.

They stumbled around drunkenly in the snow for a few moments, trying to get back to the house. Hubert lost his footing and fell headlong down a flight of stone steps. Joachim was too drunk to care, and decided to leave him there. But as he turned, he was confronted by a huge wolf, with glowing eyes. He knew in an instant that this was no ordinary wolf, it was the *loup-garou*. He fell to his knees crying, "May God have mercy on me." He felt something sharp at his back. It was a sickle hanging on a nail in the wall. He grabbed the tool and swung it at the wolf's head. Then everything went black.

When Joachim regained consciousness, he found Hubert standing over him and throwing water on him. He also saw that the hired hand had a deep gash over his ear. "You're bleeding, Hubert," he cried. "What happened?"

"Don't you remember?" said the hired hand. "Two days ago I fell in the mill and struck my head on a bucket."

The miller knew that had never happened, and he now realized what really had happened. "It was you, Hubert!" he shouted. "You are the *loup-garou*." He fell back unconscious again, and when he recovered he was raving mad. He died a few months later, and his mill was swept away in the spring floods.

➜ From the island of Usedom, off the northern coast of Germany, there is the story of the couple who were part of a group that was cutting hay in a field. The woman told her husband that she had to go away. But she made her husband promise that if any sort of wild animal came his way, he would throw his hat at it and run. Then he would not be harmed. It was a strange request, but he agreed. She had been gone only a short time when a large wolf came swimming across the river and made directly for those who were working in the fields. The man threw his hat at the animal, which instantly tore it to bits. In the meantime, a boy with a pitchfork crept up behind the wolf and stabbed it. At that moment, the wolf was transformed, and everyone saw that the boy had killed the man's wife.

➤ Even the Dutch have their werewolves. An archer was on his way to attend a shooting match at Rousse. When he had gone about halfway, he saw a large wolf spring out of a thicket and rush toward a young girl who was tending cows in a meadow. The archer didn't hesitate. He took aim, and shot the wolf in the right side. The animal howled and ran off with the arrow still sticking out of its side.

The following day, the archer heard that one of the town's leading citizens lay at the point of death from having been mysteriously shot in the side with an arrow. The archer went to the house of the wounded man and asked to see the arrow. He immediately recognized it as one of his own. He managed to talk to the wounded man alone, and got him to confess that he was indeed a werewolf and had killed and eaten many children. On the following day the man who had been a werewolf died from his wound.

7

The Werewolf and the Priest

➤ Unlike the vampire, which is almost always evil, there are a number of tales of good, or at least innocent and blameless, werewolves. These are individuals who, through no fault of their own, become trapped in the wolf form. One of the strangest of all werewolf tales of this type comes from the works of a monk named Giraldus Cambrensis. (The name translated into English means Gerald the Welshman.) In the year 1187, he wrote a book about Ireland, which he insisted contained nothing but true and authentic accounts.

"About three years before the arrival of Earl

John in Ireland," Giraldus began, "it chanced that a priest, who was journeying from Ulster towards Meath, stopped by a certain wood on the borders of Meath."

The priest was accompanied by a young lad, and the two were sitting one evening by a fire that they had just started when a wolf came up to them and said:

"Rest secure, and be not afraid, for there is no reason you should fear, where no fear is!"

The travelers were astonished by these words, and even more astonished when the wolf then uttered a prayer.

The priest implored the animal not to hurt them, and then he asked the beast what manner of creature he was that he was able to speak.

The wolf replied very courteously:

"There are two of us, a man and a woman, natives of Ossory, who through the curse of one Natalis, are compelled every seven years to put off the human form, and leave the dwellings of men. We take the form of wolves. At the end of seven years, they who chance to survive are able to return to their human shape and their home, and two others are substituted in their place." According to Giraldus, this Natalis was no evil wizard; he was a saintly man who had cursed all the people of Ossory for their sinful ways and for the stubborn persistence of pagan beliefs among them.

"And now," continued the wolf, "she who is my partner in this curse lies dangerously sick not far from here. She is at the point of death and I beseech you, inspired by divine charity, to give her the consolations of your priestly office."

The priest was moved by this tale, but still he was suspicious. He followed the wolf, but he was trembling with fear. He knew that demons could lay many snares, even for the holiest of men.

The wolf led the priest a short distance to a hollow, where a female wolf lay under a tree. The wolf looked gravely ill and was giving off almost human sighs and groans. But when the sick wolf saw the priest, she greeted him with great courtesy, and thanked him for coming to her in her hour of need.

The priest began to perform the last rites of the Church over the dying wolf, yet he was reluctant to complete these rites, which were meant for human beings, not for an animal. The male wolf begged him to go on, but the priest still hesitated.

"To remove all doubt [the wolf], using his claw for a hand, tore off the skin of the she-wolf, from the head down to the navel, folding it back. Thus she immediately presented the form of an old woman. The priest, seeing this, and compelled by his fear more than his reason, gave communion . . . afterwards, the he-wolf rolled back the skin, and fitted it to its original form."

When the rites were completed, the male wolf accompanied the priest and the boy back to the fire, and stayed with them the entire night, "behaving more like a man than a beast." In the morning the wolf led them out of the woods, and even pointed out the best road for them to take to continue their journey.

This was not just a fabulous fairy story for the people of the time, as the rest of Giraldus's narrative points out, it was a story the people believed and one which had serious implications. Giraldus says that some two years after this event was supposed to have taken place, he was passing through Meath. At that time there was a meeting of all of the leading churchmen of the region that had been called specifically to discuss the priest's account of his encounter with the human wolf.

The bishop heard that the learned Giraldus was nearby and he sent two of his clerks to ask him, "if possible to be personally present when a matter of so much importance was under consideration."

Giraldus had other urgent business to attend to, so could not appear at the meeting in person. However, he did write a long letter in which he cited a great deal of evidence proving that human beings could, under certain circumstances, appear to be transformed into animals. He quoted the great St. Augustine who wrote of the Arcadians (people of central Greece), "who were chosen by lot, swam across a lake and were there changed into wolves, living with wild beasts of the same species in the deserts of that country. If, however, they did not devour human flesh, after nine years they swam back across the lake and reassumed human form."

St. Augustine continued, "I myself, at the time I was in Italy, heard it said of some district in those parts, that there the stable-women, who had learnt magical arts, were wont to give something to travelers in their cheese which transformed them into beasts of burden." The minds of those transformed remained human and rational and when they had completed their tasks they were returned, unharmed, to their human form.

"In our time," Giraldus wrote, "we have seen persons who, by magical arts, turned any substance about them into fat pigs, as they appeared (but they were always red), and sold them in the markets. However, they disappeared as soon as they crossed any water, returning to their real nature, and with whatever care they were kept, their assumed form did not last beyond three days."

Giraldus did not believe that such transformations were "real," that is, that the essential nature of the person had been changed into that of an animal. A real transformation could be brought about only by God, not by "demons or wicked men." But he said that as a result of magical spells and incantations "the senses of men being deceived and laid asleep . . . things are not seen as they actually exist, but are strangely drawn . . . to rest their eyes on unreal and fictitious forms."

In twelfth-century Ireland, werewolves were serious business.

8

The
Noble Werewolf

In the twelfth century, a woman called Marie of France was writing tales which became very popular in the English court. One of her best-known stories concerns a very noble and grievously wronged werewolf. Marie's story was certainly based on much older tales and beliefs—most stories of this period were. Originality was not considered a virtue for a writer, and after Marie wrote it down, this story was reused in various forms by later storytellers. It can even be found among the adventures connected with King Arthur. But Marie of France's version was the first to be written down and remains the most famous.

The story was set in the French province of Brittany, a land where belief in the werewolf, called *bisclavart* in the province, was strong.

"It is a certain thing, and within the knowledge of all, that many a christened man has suffered this change, and ran wild in the woods, as a werewolf. The werewolf is a fearsome beast. He lurks within the thick forest, mad and horrible to see. All the evil that he may, he does. He goeth to and fro, about the solitary place, seeking man, in order to devour him."

That's how Marie's story begins. But, in fact, the werewolf in this story is no ravening killer.

In Brittany there was a noble baron who was held in great esteem by everyone who knew him. He was married to a beautiful and worthy lady whom he loved, and who loved him. There was only one problem with this idyllic picture; for three days every week the baron disappeared. He never told anyone where he was going, or why, and being a powerful nobleman, he didn't have to explain his actions to anyone, including his wife.

Still these unexplained absences began to prey upon his wife's mind. Finally, she told him how fearful she became every time he disappeared. "Very quickly shall I die for reason of my dread. Tell me now, where you go, and on what business. How may the knowledge of one who loves so closely bring you to harm?"

The baron resisted. "Wife, nothing but evil can come if I tell you this secret. For the mercy of God, do not require it of me. If you but knew, you would withdraw yourself from my love, and I should be lost indeed."

His wife, however, persisted and finally she wore him down.

"Wife, I become *bisclavart*. I enter in the forest, and live on prey and roots, within the thickest of the wood."

More questions followed this startling revelation.

She asked whether he wore clothes while he was in his wolf form.

"Wife," said he, "I go naked as a beast."

"Tell me, what do you do with your clothing?"

At that point, the baron resisted. "Fair wife, that I will never tell you. If I should lose my clothing, then I would be a werewolf for all the days of my life. Never again should I become a man, save in that hour my clothing were given back to me. For this reason I will never reveal my lair."

But the lady persisted. "Why do you doubt me? For what sin do you mistrust my honor? Open your heart, and tell me."

And so the baron finally gave in.

"Wife, within this wood, there is a little path and at the end of it is an ancient chapel. Nearby is a great hollow stone, concealed by a bush, and there is the secret place where I hide my clothing until I can return to my own home."

Though the lady professed her love for her husband in spite of his terrible secret, she was in reality quite nervous about being married to a werewolf. And she began to hatch a scheme to get rid of her shape-shifting husband.

There was a certain knight who had loved the lady for years. But he had never been given so much as a word of encouragement. Now she wrote to him:

"Fair friend, be happy. That which you have coveted so long a time I will grant you. Never again will I deny your suit. My heart, and all I have to give are yours."

After receiving an oath of loyalty from the love-stricken knight, the lady explained the situation to him. She showed him the chapel and the hollow stone, and explained how the werewolf would not be able to return to human form if his clothes were stolen. It is not difficult to imagine what they plotted to do. And the next time the baron went away, he did not return.

His complete disappearance came as a great shock to his relatives and many friends. They searched everywhere for him, but not a trace of him could they find. After a decent interval, everyone assumed that the baron had died somehow. And the lady married the knight who had helped her.

More than a year after the disappearance, the king came to hunt in the forest where the werewolf lived. The king's hounds quickly picked up the wolf's scent, and soon the whole pack was chasing him.

The hounds wore the wolf down. Just as they seemed to be closing in for the kill, the wolf saw the king, seated on his horse nearby. He ran to the king, took his stirrup in his paws and licked the king's boot.

At first the king was frightened. But he soon got over his fear, and called all the others in his party to come and see "this marvelous thing." The king declared, "Here is a beast who has the sense of man. He surrenders to his enemy, and cries for mercy, although he cannot speak. Beat off the hounds, and let no man do him harm. We will hunt no more today, but return to our own palace, with the wonderful quarry we have taken."

As the king turned and rode home, the werewolf followed closely at his side, like a faithful dog. At the palace this astonishingly intelligent and apparently tame wolf became a source of great pride for the king. "He held him so dear, that he bade all those who wished for his love to cross the Wolf in naught, neither to strike him with a rod, but ever to see that he was richly fed and kennelled warm."

The king's orders were obeyed to the letter. "There was not a man who did not make much of the beast, so frank was he and debonair." The werewolf slept at the foot of the king's bed, and during the day went everywhere with him. "All perceived that the king loved him as his friend."

One day the king called all his lords and barons to a great feast. Among those who were called was the knight who had married the werewolf's lady. He came to the castle wearing his finest clothes, and surrounded by a retinue of servants. But the minute he entered the great hall the werewolf charged at him "and seized him with his fangs, in the king's very presence and to the view of all."

The werewolf would doubtless have killed the man, if he had not been pulled off. The king was astonished. Up to that very moment the wolf had never shown hostility toward anyone. The king decided that the wolf must have suffered some bitter wrong at the hand of the knight, but he had no idea what that might be. For his part, the knight stayed as far away from the wolf as he possibly could, and left the castle at the first opportunity. He was glad to get out with his life.

A short time later the king again went hunting in that forest where he had first encountered the werewolf. With the king came the wolf, and a large company of friends and servants also accompanied him.

The king spent the night at a lodge in the woods. The lady, who had once been the wife of the werewolf, lived quite nearby. She heard of the king's arrival, and in the morning went directly to the lodge in order to pay her respects and present the king with a gift, as was customary. But the moment she entered the chamber, the wolf went mad with fury. He broke away from those who were attempting to restrain him, threw himself upon the lady and bit her nose off. The king's servants managed to beat the wolf off before he killed her.

They would have cut the wolf to pieces, but they were restrained by the king. One of the king's wisest counsellors put two and two together and said:

"Sire, hearken now to me. The beast is always with you, and there is not one amongst us who has not known him for long. He goes in and out amongst us, nor has molested any man, neither done wrong or felony to any, save only to this dame, one only time as we have seen. He has done evil to this lady, and to that knight, who is now the husband of the dame. Sire, she was once the wife of a lord who was close to you, but who went, and none might find where he has gone."

He suggested that he take the lady away and "question her straitly"—that meant under torture—to find out if she knew why the wolf hated her so. "For many a strange deed has chanced, as well we know, in this marvellous land of Brittany."

So the woman was taken away, and eventually she told them what she knew. She told them how her husband, the werewolf, had been betrayed when his clothes were stolen from the hollow stone. She never saw him again, but was now convinced that he was the king's wolf.

The king demanded that the stolen clothes be brought to him. They were then spread in front of the wolf, but the animal paid no attention to them. The counsellor thought he knew why.

He said that the wolf would be ashamed to carry out the transformation from animal back to human "in the sight of all." He suggested, "Carry your wolf within your most secret chamber, and put his clothes therein. Then close the door upon him, and leave him alone for a space. So we shall see presently whether the ravening beast may indeed return to human shape."

The king took the wolf to his chamber and shut the doors. After a while he went back to the room accompanied by two lords. The three entered the room quietly and found the missing baron sleeping in the king's bed, "like a little child." There was no sign of the wolf.

The king was overjoyed to see his old friend again. "When the man's speech returned once more, he told him of his adventure. Then the king restored to his friend the lands that were stolen from him, and gave such rich gifts moreover, as I cannot tell. As for the wife who had betrayed the werewolf, he bade her to avoid his country and chased her from the realm. So she went forth, she and her second lord together, to seek a more abiding city, and were seen no more."

Marie of France concludes her story with these words:

"The adventure you have heard is no vain fable. Verily and indeed it chanced as I have said."

9

The Werewolf's Ghost

➤ In the early years of this century an Englishwoman named Miss St. Denis had a very curious and frightening tale to relate.

She was staying at a farm in the rugged area of Wales called Merlonethshire. The farm was a considerable distance from the nearest village, but it was within easy walking distance of a tiny railway station. There were few trains through the area, the station had only one employee, and was often completely unattended.

The station platform commanded a very good view of the surrounding countryside. Miss St. Denis was an amateur artist and she regularly went down to the station with her sketchbook.

On one occasion she became deeply absorbed in her work, and stayed on later than she had intended, until the sun was beginning to set. As she prepared to leave she saw what she took to be the figure of a man sitting on one of the carts used to move freight to and from the train. The sight surprised her. Except on the rare occasions when a train stopped she had never seen anybody at the station except the stationmaster. And by this late in the day the station was invariably deserted. The unexpected appearance of a strange figure suddenly made her feel uneasy.

For the first time, Miss St. Denis realized just how deserted and gloomy the place really was. The stationmaster lived in a little house several hundred yards away. Aside from that dwelling, the closest house was at the farm where she was staying. That was several miles away. Suddenly the cliffs looked shadowy and forbidding in the fading light. Here and there were the gaping and gloomy entrances to abandoned slate quarries. Piles of rock fragments were heaped around the entrances. The only vegetation were drawfed and gnarled trees. It was not a beautiful scene, but it was one which had fascinated Miss St. Denis—until now. The strange figure and the gathering darkness frightened her.

She couldn't make the figure out clearly in the

dim light, but she was uncomfortably aware of one thing—it seemed to have unpleasantly bright eyes, and it was staring at her.

Miss St. Denis tried to act casually. She gathered up her campstool and drawing things, and then she coughed loudly, to see if it would have any effect on the silent figure. It didn't. She coughed again. And again there was no response. Then she said, "Could you tell me the time, please?" but there was still no reply. The figure just sat there staring at her with its unnaturally bright eyes.

She picked up her things and walked off the station platform, trying to look as if nothing at all was wrong, though she felt that something was terribly wrong. She glanced quickly over her shoulder and saw what she expected, and feared. The figure was following her. She tried even harder to appear unworried and casual—she even began to whistle what she hoped sounded like a cheery tune, but she also started walking faster. The figure was still following with long easy strides, and it was getting closer.

Very soon she knew that she would reach the worst part of the road home. There were cliffs on either side and by this time it would be pitch black. "Indeed, the spot positively invited murder, and she might shriek herself hoarse without the remotest chance of making herself heard," wrote the man who later recorded this strange tale.

Miss St. Denis realized that she could no longer just ignore the odd figure that was so obviously stalking her. She gathered up all her courage, swung around, and shouted, "What do you want? How dare you—" She got no further. The figure was quite close now, and it was illuminated by the last rays of the dying sun. Miss St. Denis got her first good look at what was following her, and she discovered to her absolute horror that it was not a man, it was not human at all.

The body was greyish, and generally human in form, but the head was very clearly that of a wolf. It tensed up its muscles as if it were about to spring. Almost instinctively, Miss St. Denis reached into the pocket of her jacket where she carried a small flashlight. She switched it on and shone the light in the creature's face. It was as if she had waved a magic wand. The creature shrank back, and threw its paw-like hands over its face as if to shield its eyes from the light. Then it simply disappeared.

Later, she made discreet inquiries, but she was able to learn nothing except that in one of the quarries near the station some curious bones, part animal, part human, had once been found. She was also told that local people always shunned the area after dusk, though no one was sure why or when the tradition had started.

Miss St. Denis believed that she had seen the ghost of a werewolf.

➤ This very strange story was collected by a man named Elliott O'Donnell. For many years, O'Donnell, a tall striking-looking Irishman, was the foremost collector of ghostly accounts in the British Isles, and the author of numerous books on the subject. But along with the tales of grey ladies and spectral knights gliding down dusty castle corridors, O'Donnell encountered stories of other apparently supernatural appearances. Indeed, in 1912 he published an entire book devoted to stories of encounters with werewolves in one form or another. Miss St. Denis' story, which she told directly to O'Donnell, is from that book. Here is another.

This story was told to O'Donnell in 1910 by a family named Anderson. The Andersons had come into a good deal of money. They bought some land in Cumberland County, in the northwest of England, and had a big stone house built for themselves and their three young children.

The house was extremely comfortable, but it was isolated, and soon they began to have trouble keeping servants. The servants said that they didn't like living in such a lonely spot, and that they were being kept awake by strange noises that they heard at night. Mr. and Mrs. Anderson heard nothing, and at first they thought the servants were just making up stories about strange noises as an excuse for quitting. But then the children began to complain about the noises.

"What sort of noises are they?" the Andersons asked.

"Wild animals," said Willie, the eldest child. "They come howling round the window at night, and we hear their feet patter along the passage and stop at our door."

Puzzled, and more than a little alarmed, the Andersons decided to sit up with their children at night and listen. At about two or three in the morning the noises began. At first, it was a growling sound beneath the window. Mr. Anderson had lived in Canada for a while, and he was familiar with the noises made by wolves. This sounded like the growling of a wolf, right under the window. He threw open the window and peered out. The moon was very bright and the whole area was clearly illuminated, but he could see nothing that could have made the noises—not a wolf, or any other kind of animal. And as soon as the window was opened, the noises stopped. But when the window was closed, they started again. Once again Mr. Anderson went to the window—nothing.

After a while the growling noises stopped, and the Andersons heard something more ominous, the sound of the front door, which they had carefully locked, being opened. Then there were the footsteps, not human footsteps but those of a large, soft-footed animal, coming up the stairs. Mr. Anderson waited until the steps were just outside the room, then he threw open the door and thrust his lamp into the hall. The hall was empty.

The next morning the Andersons searched all around the house. They couldn't find a trace of footprints, or anything else to indicate what had made the noises in the night. Now they were more puzzled than frightened.

Several weeks went by and the noises were not heard again. While they didn't exactly forget about the experience, the Andersons became completely absorbed in something else. It was getting close to Christmas, their first Christmas in the new house, and they were determined to make it the best Christmas they ever had. The setting, a large house in the country, was certainly perfect for a big Christmas celebration.

Mr. Anderson had a special surprise planned. When he had asked his children what they wanted Santa Claus to bring them for Christmas, he had been told in no uncertain terms that there was no Santa Claus. The youngest child even threatened to stick a pin in the jolly old elf if he showed up!

Mr. Anderson was determined to thwart this youthful cynicism. He had secretly purchased a full

Santa Claus costume, with which he intended to surprise his children on Christmas Eve.

The day before Christmas came just as the Andersons would have hoped, with a new snowfall. The
children were sent up to bed at about ten, though no
one thought that they were going to go to sleep. At
midnight, Mr. Anderson, in full Santa Claus regalia,
walked into the hallway which led to the children's
bedroom. He was almost staggering under the
weight of an enormous sackful of presents. "It's going
to be a perfect Christmas," he thought.

If Mr. Anderson had known more about werewolf lore, he might not have been quite so confident.
Myths and legends from many countries associate
werewolves with the Christmas season. That knowledge, plus the recent experience with the wolf noises
and padding footsteps, should have put him on his
guard.

There was no thought of werewolves in his mind
as he headed for the children's room—until he heard
the faint sound of yelping. It was undoubtedly a wolf
noise—yet there was something not quite wolfish
about it, something almost human. He kept walking
down the hall, and the noise got nearer. By the time
he had reached the door to the children's room he was
sweating with fear, and his knees were shaking. The
noise was much closer and it had changed to a moan-

ing, snarling, drawn-out cry that ended in a whine.

The clock began striking twelve midnight, and Mr. Anderson entered the children's room, trying to look jolly. But a huge grey shadowy figure entered right behind him. The children were fully awake now, and they stared at two strange figures in the middle of the room. One was a very frightened-looking Santa Claus. The other, greyish and much taller, looked something like a man with the head of a wolf, with sharp white teeth and glowing eyes. It was quite obvious why Santa Claus looked so frightened.

It's impossible to know how long this standoff would have lasted, or what would have happened next. Mrs. Anderson, who wanted to see how her husband's impersonation of Santa Claus was being received, decided to visit the children's room. She didn't like the idea of walking down corridors illumi-nated only by the moonlight, so she carried a candle. She opened the door to the children's room and thrust the candle inside. As the candlelight fell on the wolf-thing, the figure vanished.

"Why, whatever were you all doing?" she asked innocently.

Everybody began talking at once. The sack full of presents tumbled to the floor unnoticed. Every can-dle and lamp in the house was lit, and no one slept that Christmas Eve. They just huddled together in the best-lighted spot they could find. The following morning the Andersons decided that the house should be put up for sale or rent at the earliest possible opportunity. A search of the grounds, however, revealed no wolf footprints, or anything else suspicious in the new-fallen snow.

Fortunately for the Andersons, they were able to rent the house after only a few weeks. Before leaving, Mr. Anderson made another exhaustive search of his property. In a cave behind the house he found a number of bones. They appeared to be the remains of a human skeleton with the skull missing. Mixed among the human bones was the skull of a wolf. Mr. Anderson burned the bones, hoping that by this act he would rid the house of its unwelcome visitor. There were no further reports of wolfish noises or the strange figure.

➤ Elliott O'Donnell had one more curious tale of this type to relate. He heard it from a Mr. Warren, who had grown up on the Hebrides, those wild and bleak islands off the coast of Scotland.

When Warren was a teenager, he lived with his grandfather, a man who was very interested in natural science. The old man had filled the house with all manner of fossils and strange rocks collected from the area. One morning he came home in a great state of excitement, and dragged the boy out to show him what he had found at the bottom of a dried-up lake.

"Look!" he cried, bending down and pointing at some bones. "Here is a human skeleton with a wolf's head. What do you make of it?"

The boy didn't know what to make of it.

"It's a werewolf," cried the old man. "This island was once overrun with werewolves."

They carried the remains home and put them on a table in one of the back rooms. That evening young Warren was left alone while the rest of the family went to church. He sat and read for a while, but then thought he heard a noise coming from the back of the house. He explored the room in which the werewolf's bones were laid out, but could find nothing, and so he decided that the noise had been made by a rat.

He sat down at the table that held the bones, and waited to see if the noises would start again. For a while all was quiet. Then there was the sound of loud rapping on one of the windows.

"I immediately turned in the direction of the noise and encountered, to my alarm, a dark face looking in at me. At first dim and indistinct, it became more and more complete, until it developed into a very perfectly defined head of a wolf ending in the neck of a human being."

The boy was badly frightened, but he looked around to see if there was any way that this strange vision could be a reflection in the glass, or some other sort of illusion. He saw nothing, and decided it was real.

"I looked at the face and marked each feature intently. It was unmistakably a wolf's face, the jaws slightly distended; the lips wreathed in a savage snarl; the teeth sharp and white; the eyes light green; the ears pointed. The expression of the face was diabolically malignant, and as it gazed straight at me my horror was as intense as my wonder. This it seemed to notice, for a look of savage exultation crept into its eyes, and it raised one hand—a slender hand, like that of a woman, though with prodigiously long and curved fingernails—menacingly, as if about to dash in the windowpane."

He remembered what his grandfather had told him about evil spirits, and he crossed himself. But that didn't seem to have any effect. So he ran out of the room, locking the door behind him, and spent the next hour or so cowering in the hallway.

When his family returned, they were extremely upset by what they heard. The next morning they carried the bones out of the house, and buried them just where they had been found.

And they may still lie there today.

10

The Werewolf in Washington Square

➤ In the twentieth, or soon to be twenty-first, century the transformation of a man (or woman) into a wolf may seem farfetched, and unbelievable. But the idea that someone might come to believe that they had been changed, or that someone would become possessed by some sort of animal spirit, it not quite so far outside of what we in a modern, rational age might consider possible.

Certainly the writer William Seabrook did not consider such a transformation beyond the realm of possibility. Seabrook spent most of his career looking for strange, unusual, and often terrifying events to write about—and he often found them. In 1929 he wrote an extremely popular book called *Voodoo Island* about voodoo in Haiti. But he reported on many bizarre happenings in this country as well.

In his 1940 book, *Witchcraft*, Seabrook described a scene that he had personally witnessed in the 1920s in New York City's Washington Square area. At that time Washington Square was the heart of Greenwich Village and a magnet for painters, writers, and others involved in the arts. As in most artistic communities, the residents would often become interested in unconventional beliefs.

In the 1920s, some of the Greenwich Villagers were first introduced to the *I Ching*, the *Book of Changes*, a very ancient and extremely obscure Chinese work. And changes, often from man to animal, is what this book is all about. Here is a verse from it:

> *The common man may change his face; the sage may change his whole being as does the leopard.*
> *Two sisters may live together in the same skin, differing and opposed, yet the same.*
> *The great sage may change himself as the tiger changes its form and stripes.*

You may find the words puzzling. Don't be embarrassed. I freely admit that I do not understand the significance of this particular verse, called the *ko hexagram*, either. I have only the foggiest notion of the purpose of the *I Ching* itself, and I've read, or tried to read, the whole thing.

But we are in good company in our ignorance. James Legge, a celebrated Oriental scholar who first translated the work into English, said that when he finished his translation, he still didn't understand it either. "[I] have to acknowledge that when the manuscript [his translation of the *I Ching*] was completed, I knew very little about the scope and methods of the book. I laid the volumes containing the result of my labor aside, and hoped, believed, indeed that the light would by and by dawn and that I should one day get hold of a clue that would guide me to a knowledge of the mysterious classic."

Legge said that it was another twenty years before he got even a glimmering of an idea of what the *I Ching* was supposed to mean. And then he was never able to transmit his understanding successfully to his Western readers.

The greatest and most influential of all Chinese scholars, Confucius himself, edited and wrote commentaries on the *I Ching*. Confucius lived in the fifth century B.C. and the book was ancient even in his day. What is more, Confucius, the most respected of all Chinese sages, had trouble understanding what it meant. But the book fascinated him. He reportedly once said that he wished that he had fifty years more of life to study the classic.

The *I Ching* is, on its most basic level, a book of divination—fortune-telling. There are special *I Ching* coins, which are thrown on the ground, and the pattern in which they land is what must be interpreted. This is by no means as easy as it sounds, for the interpretations are obscure and mystical and for most raised in the West, quite impossible to grasp.

English translations of the *I Ching* began appearing in the United States in the early 1920s, and trying to divine the future by tossing *I Ching* coins and interpreting their pattern became popular, even though most of the people who tried the system hadn't the faintest notion of what it was they were doing.

Interest in such exotic practices usually begins among artistic types, like those who lived in the Washington Square area during the 1920s. And that brings us back to William Seabrook and his werewolf. He described a scene that he observed in a Greenwich Village apartment. A group of individuals who were interested in the exotic and occult were experimenting with the *I Ching*. They were meditating on the *ko hexagram* which was quoted earlier. The translation of the explanation of the hexagram makes it sound as if some sort of transformation, perhaps even a change from human to animal, is being discussed. That probably is not what it means, but that's what it sounds like.

One of the group in the apartment was a young Russian woman Seabrook called Nastatia Fillipovna. He described her as a "neurasthentic, hyperimaginative type, already addicted to occult escape mechanisms."

After a few hours of meditation, Nastatia began to mutter about running through the snow on her hands and feet. "She was breathing heavily, panting. Her big, handsome mouth was open, drooling, and when she next broke the silence, it was with sounds that were not human. There were yelps, slavering, panting, and the deep baying such as only two sorts of animals on earth emit when they are running — hounds and wolves."

Others in the room who were witnessing this scene became alarmed at this strange and ferocious behavior. One of the men tried to get her to snap out of her trancelike state. "The girl snarled hideously, her eyes wide open now, and leaped for his throat," wrote Seabrook. "She would have torn his throat with her teeth if the long-crouched position had not numbed her so that she lurched and fell heavily. And now, literally on all fours crawling, she slithered, still snarling, into the dark shadows of the corner." Some-what later Nastatia awoke and said that she remembered nothing of what had happened.

At one time such a display of wolflike behavior could have gotten the young woman into serious trouble. In New York of the 1920s, it was merely passed off as a curious incident. But it is a dramatic example of how an ordinary person can convince himself or herself that a transformation into a wolf has taken place.

11

Werewolves and How to Know Them

➤ In its animal form, the werewolf was fairly easy to recognize. It looked like a wolf, or something like a wolf. It might be bigger or have a stumpy tail or no tail at all, and its eyes often seemed to glow. Or it might look like a combination of man and wolf, most commonly a human body with a wolf's head. Whatever it looked like, it was always fiercer, more intelligent, and infinitely more danger- ous than a "natural" wolf.

In human form, however, the werewolf was not so easy to recognize. In the werewolf trials, the ac- cused were usually pretty disreputable-looking individuals. They were covered with scratches and wounds from running through the forest and being attacked by dogs while in their wolf form. They tended to have long, matted hair and beards, sharp teeth, and even in human form might run about on all fours, barking and baying at the moon. Any disfigured individual might fall under suspicion. Henri Boguet, a judge who tried many werewolf cases, said that one celebrated werewolf "was so much disfigured . . . that he bore hardly any resemblance to a man, and struck with horror those who looked at him."

But other werewolves had to be recognized by more subtle signs. Any evil-looking person might be suspected, particularly if the person had bushy eyebrows that met in the middle of his forehead. In his *The Book of Werewolves*, Sabine Baring-Gould says:

"A werewolf may easily be detected, even when devoid of his skin; for his hands are broad, and his fingers short, and there are always some hairs in the hollow of his hand."

Hairy palms was considered an unmistakable sign of the werewolf condition. For that reason, real werewolves would often shave their palms. But this left the palms of the hands rough, and so rough skin on the palm was considered another sign. Having a pentagram or five-pointed star, a satanic symbol, appear in the palm is Hollywood lore, rather than authentic werewolf folklore. The pentagram first appears in the film *The Wolf Man*. In the film the werewolf was also supposed to be able to see the pentagram in the palm of his next victim.

In some parts of the world a sure sign that a person was a werewolf was that the third finger of the person's hand was longer than his middle finger. Peter Fleming's classic werewolf story, *The Kill*, contains this description:

"The stranger's smile was now a grin, a ravening convulsion of the face. His eyes blazed with a hard and purposeful delight. A thread of saliva dangled from the corner of his mouth.

"Very slowly he lifted one hand and removed his bowler hat. Of the fingers crooked about its brim, the third was longer than the second."

Another belief was that while in human form the werewolf wore his skin inside out. It looked like ordinary human skin, but the fur grew on the inside. In 1541, a madman was caught who told his captors that he was a werewolf, but his pelt was inside out. To find out if he was telling the truth, the authorities cut off his arms and legs. After the experiment they decided that he did not have fur growing on the inside, and therefore he was innocent. But by that time the self-confessed werewolf had already bled to death.

Some werewolves are hard to miss in any form.

In the dramatist John Webster's seventeenth-century horror/shocker play, *The Duchess of Malfi*, among the bizarre and terrible characters there is a duke who robs graves and goes around carrying a dead man's leg on his shoulder. When asked about this odd ornament, one of the characters says that the duke is suffering from "a very pestilent disease, my lord. They call it lycanthropia."

While most werewolves were considered active predators, that is, in their wolf form they pursued and killed sheep, cattle, and people, there is also a body of tradition which holds that the werewolf can be a scavenger, a grave robber as well as a killer, like the mad duke in Webster's play.

In the French province of Normandy, there is a traditional belief in strange wolflike creatures called *lupins* or *lubins*. They spend the nights huddled by the walls of country cemeteries. They appear to be talking together in some unknown language, and often they howl dismally at the moon. In most parts of Normandy they are supposed to be very shy and fearful, and will run when anyone approaches. But in some districts they are believed to be quite fierce, and dig up graves to gnaw upon the bones of the dead.

There were many ways to become a werewolf. As we have seen, the popular modern notion that a person became a werewolf after being bitten by another werewolf is really an invention of the movies. In real life, or at least in traditional belief, a person became a werewolf after making some sort of pact with the devil. Francesco-Maria Guazzo, an Italian monk who wrote extensively on the subject of witchcraft and other diabolical activities during the early seventeenth century, had this to say about werewolves:

"Just as emperors reserve certain rewards for their veteran soldiers only, so the demon grants the power of changing themselves into different shapes, as the witches believe, only to those who have proved their loyalty by many years of faithful service in witchcraft; and this is as it were a reward for their long service and loyalty."

Typically, the devil would give his servant a magic salve to rub on or a magic garment, usually made of wolfskin, to wear. But the idea of the transformation taking place at the time of the full moon is not just a Hollywood invention. The full moon was always associated with violent madness—hence the words *lunacy* and *lunatic* (*luna* is Latin for moon).

There were long and complicated spells for turning men into wolves to be found in some of the medieval *grimories* or books on magic. These involved bubbling cauldrons of disgusting ingredients, long incomprehensible chants, magic circles, and all of the other trappings of ceremonial magic. Aside from a garment of wolfskin, a belt made of human skin, preferably from the skin of an executed criminal, might bring about the transformation. It was widely believed that anyone who tasted human flesh might become a werewolf. Indeed, anyone who was sinful or had been excommunicated by the Church stood in mortal danger of becoming a werewolf.

The peasants also thought that a man could become a wolf by eating roasted wolf flesh, wearing or smelling the plant wolfbane, drinking from certain enchanted streams or pools, or by drinking rainwater that had collected in the footprint of a savage wolf. Serious students of the werewolf, however, knew that all such beliefs were ignorant superstitions. A person became a werewolf only by dealing directly with the devil.

In order to get rid of a werewolf, silver bullets were always good. Silver was the "moon metal" and since werewolves came out at the time of the full moon, there was a magical connection. As we have seen, cutting off the limb of a werewolf was also effective. But the time-honored way of getting rid of a werewolf was by burning. Not only did this kill the living werewolf, the method made sure that the werewolf would not come back as something else after death, for there was a tradition that a dead werewolf would come back as a vampire. No one wanted to go through all the trouble of getting rid of a living monster just to be plagued by an undead one.

As with most other newsgroups and networks, you can be anonymous if you wish. You can adopt a pseudonym. Those on the werewolf net tend to favor lupine or exotic names like Volk, Vladwolf, Katmandu, and Lord Kelkemen. Most of the messages appear to be sent through university computer systems. Some have disclaimers saying that the views expressed are not necessarily those of the computer owner.

AHWW, according to its FAQ (Frequently Asked Question) sheet, was a newsgroup originally created to discuss horror genre fiction dealing with werewolves. But it rapidly expanded into a discussion of all aspects of werewolves and lycanthropy. In fact, there was a discussion about renaming the group to get out of the horror genre. But it was finally decided that a name change would be too difficult and too many people might lose access to the group. So alt.horror.werewolves it remains, though the title is no longer entirely accurate. This is not really a horror story or film fan group anymore. It is a werewolf group.

There is discussion of comic books where werewolves figure as characters, and some of the more popular fantasy role-playing games—werewolves or other shapeshifters show up frequently in the games. There is also some talk of rock music, mainly heavy metal—werewolf themes can be found in some of the lyrics. But most of the messages are about were-wolves themselves, what they are, and what they can and can't do.

It's not that all of those on AHWW believe that they actually are werewolves, or even that it is possible for *anyone* to physically change from human to wolf, or any other sort of animal. But most are more than willing to entertain that possibility. "Most of the individuals on AHWW probably haven't ever shifted, but who's to say?" says one. It is quite clear that most of them would like to.

Not all the discussions are serious. There are the jokes — I like the top ten lists. On the top ten list of reasons for having a werewolf for a pet: They can fool landlords who have a "no pet" policy, and if they can't fool the landlord, they can always eat him. One of the top ten disadvantages is that the shower drain is always getting clogged with hair. The top disadvantage, according to this list, is that the werewolf hogs the computer and is always accessing AHWW.

What do you do if you meet a werewolf and want to avoid being eaten? "Throw a stick and shout, 'Fetch.'" "Point in one direction and say, 'Look, it's Elvis!' and run the opposite way."

On a more serious, and a more personal level, members of this newsgroup — the more involved call it a pack or cyberpack — discuss their devotion to, and perhaps obsession with, the idea of the werewolf.

One regarded himself as a "spiritual werewolf" who had as yet been unable to unlock the secrets of physical transformation. "Though, I have come pretty close at times."

I did, however, get in contact with one individual who claimed to regularly undergo a physical transformation into wolf form. He described his first transformation—which took place when he was sixteen—in considerable detail for me.

It came upon him quite unexpectedly. He was sitting alone by a river one evening when suddenly, "Certain parts of my body felt different, or even in the wrong place! . . . It was kinda strange getting used to a new body."

During the transformation he resumed what he calls his "natural" or wolf form, with a traditional wolf's head—ears, muzzle, whiskers, etc. "I was quite glad that I had my glasses up on my head before the change started, wonder how bad it would hurt if I had changed with them on." He found out later—it hurt a lot. As a result of the transformation, he was covered with hair or fur.

After about twenty-five minutes, he changed back again. "I was feeling confused about it and didn't really want to talk to anyone."

The transformation was not brought about by being bitten by a werewolf, having a magical or diabolical salve, or anything like that. The werewolf says that the condition must be hereditary. He never knew his father, but assumes that his werewolf nature comes from that side of the family.

This particular individual has done quite well for himself in the werewolf world. He has gathered a "pack" and calls himself an Alpha-leader, who claims a large portion of the U.S. as the pack's territory.

Leadership has its burdens and this Alpha-leader says that his pack has endured numerous "attacks" on their territory from other packs.

A common theme that ran through many of the personal stories of these Internet werewolves was the feeling of being profoundly different from others around them. Though they would like to be friendly—wolves are by nature social animals—there weren't very many of them, so they tended to be lonely. The Internet has become a place where these late-twentieth-century werewolves can be themselves, get in contact with kindred souls, and in a sense roam free.

For many in the Internet wolf pack, the transformation seems to come in dreams. But here the werewolf dreams are not of running through the forest ripping up cattle and chewing up small children. They don't see themselves as "ravening beasts," and monsters, something diabolical and unnatural. On the contrary, they think of themselves as somehow being closer to true nature than ordinary folk, who have only one shape. Their dreams are about the freedom of the natural world and the friendship and commitment of the members of the pack to one another.

There is more talk of Native American beliefs in the unity and interchangeable nature of all things than there is about wolfskin shirts and black magic.

Just as society's view of the wolf has changed from that of a fierce and dangerous adversary to that of a severely threatened symbol of the wild, so the view of werewolves may be changing as well.

These werewolves of the Internet may be the werewolves for the twenty-first century.

13

Ten Great Werewolf Films

➤ There are not nearly as many werewolf films as there are vampire films. Some of these, like *Werewolf in a Girl's Dormitory* (1961), are really, really bad, and should be seen only by those who get a kick out of really, really bad films. But there are some genuine classics as well. Here are my ten favorites ranked in order. All of them are available on videotape somewhere.

1. THE WOLF MAN (1941) Directed by George Waggner. Starring: Lon Chaney, Jr., Evelyn Ankers, Claude Rains, Marie Ouspenskaya, Ralph Bellamy,

Patric Knowles, Warren William, and Bela Lugosi.

This wasn't the first werewolf film ever made, but it set the standard for everything that followed. The real star of the film was never seen on the screen. He was Universal Studio's ace makeup artist, Jack Pierce, who created the Wolf Man look. It took about six hours to put the Wolf Man makeup on Chaney, and the transformation was shown on the screen in under a minute. But it was unforgettable. Even today, when technology allows moviemakers to create far more elaborate special effects, this one still looks good. The cast is superb, the script crisp and literate, and both scenery and the music capture the proper brooding and gloomy atmosphere. The film also features one of the most famous bits of poetry ever written for the screen:

> *Even a man who is pure at heart*
> *And says his prayers at night*
> *May become a wolf when the wolfbane blooms*
> *And the moon is full and bright.*

2. WEREWOLF OF LONDON (1935) Directed by Stuart Walker. Starring Henry Hull, Warner Oland, Valerie Hobson, Lester Matthews, Spring Byington. This *is* the first werewolf film. Hull is an innocent scientist who accidentally becomes a werewolf. He can be cured only by a rare Tibetan flower that is

also coveted by Oland, another werewolf. This film is a bit patchy, but there are some excellent suspense scenes, and it is an authentic milestone in the history of horror films.

3. AN AMERICAN WEREWOLF IN LONDON (1981) Directed by John Landis. Starring David Naughton, Jenny Agutter, Griffin Dunne, John Woodvine, Brian Glover. Two young American students are bitten by a werewolf while crossing the English moors. This film is not a spoof, it is a genuine horror film, and parts of it are truly frightening, but other parts are very, very funny. What makes the film really memorable, however, are the Oscar-winning makeup and special effects. It marks the first real improvement in these areas since Jack Pierce's Wolf Man makeup forty years earlier. The only disappointment is the final look at the werewolf itself; it's not the hairy-faced human wolf man, but is supposed to look like a real wolf. Actually, it looks like a fat German shepherd.

4. WOLF (1994) Directed by Mike Nichols. Starring Jack Nicholson, Michelle Pfeiffer, James Spader, Kate Nelligan, Christopher Plummer, Eileen Atkins. A good contemporary werewolf tale, with Nicholson as a repressed book editor who is bitten by a werewolf and undergoes a startling, and not al-

together unwelcome, change. All the old werewolf clichés are here, but they are given a modern urban setting. Nicholson is just the sort of over-the-top actor who was born to play a werewolf. If you are looking for graphic horror with severed limbs and buckets of blood, you will be disappointed. But this is an intriguing and intelligent film and a must for the connoisseur of this genre.

5. CURSE OF THE WEREWOLF (1961) Directed by Terence Fisher. Starring Clifford Evans, Oliver Reed, Yvonne Roman, Anthony Dawson. Starting in the late 1950s, Britain's Hammer Studios began remaking all of the old Universal Studio horror films, in color and with more violence and gore. This was Hammer's only venture into the werewolf genre. It's not really a remake of *The Wolf Man*, for it's set in medieval Spain, not twentieth-century England, and this werewolf was born, not created by the bite of another werewolf. The film is creepy and effective and Reed's muscular, white-furred werewolf is truly frightening.

6. WOLFEN (1981) Directed by Michael Wadleigh. Starring Albert Finney, Diane Vernoea, Edward James Olmos, Gregory Hines, Tom Noonan, Dick O'Neil. The creatures in this film are not, strictly speaking, werewolves. But they are close enough to

satisfy all but the dedicated nitpickers. A detective trying to solve a string of gruesome murders in New York City discovers a tribe of wolves specially adapted to be urban predators. It's the sort of film that will appeal to fans of TV's "X-Files."

7. THE HOWLING (1981) Directed by Joe Dante. Starring Dee Wallace, Patrick Macnee, Dennis Dugan, Christopher Stone, Belinda Balanski, Kevin McCarthy, John Carradine, Slim Pickins. A woman newscaster reporting on a strange California medical retreat discovers that most of the patients are werewolves. This film is clever, well-made, and has excellent special effects. But it is really a film for horror film buffs, because it's filled with in-jokes. For example, almost every character is named after a director of horror films.

8. ABBOTT AND COSTELLO MEET FRANKENSTEIN (1948) Directed by Charles Barton. Starring Bud Abbott, Lou Costello, Lon Chaney, Jr., Bela Lugosi, Lenore Aubert, Jan Randolph, Glenn Strange. This is the first, and best, of the "Abbott and Costello Meet the Monster" series, and quite possibly the best of the many Abbott and Costello films. Boris Karloff declined the part of the Frankenstein monster because he didn't think a comedy of this type would be

popular. (He was wrong, and did some of the later and less successful Abbott and Costello films). But Lugosi was there in his Dracula role, and Chaney as the Wolf Man had the biggest part aside from Abbott and Costello. As usual, the werewolf failed to get top billing.

9. FRANKENSTEIN MEETS THE WOLF MAN (1943) Directed by Roy William. Starring Lon Chaney, Jr., William Neil, Patric Knowles, Ilona Massey, Bela Lugosi, Maria Ouspenskaya, Lionel Atwill, Dennis Hoey, Rex Evans, Dwight Frye. This is the first sequel to *The Wolf Man*. Lawrence Talbot (the Wolf Man) travels to Vasaria to find a cure for his condition. Instead, he finds the Frankenstein monster (played by a miscast Lugosi) being reactivated. This is a stylish film that is a lot better than you might think. Definitely worth a look if you haven't seen it.

10. HOUSE OF FRANKENSTEIN (1943) Directed by Erle C. Kenton. Starring Boris Karloff, J. Carroll Naish, Lon Chaney, Jr., John Carradine, Elena Verdugo, Anne Gwynne, Lionel Atwill, Peter Coe, George Zucco, Glenn Strange, Sig Rumann. Karloff plays a mad scientist, not the monster. The picture has two parts; the first deals with Dracula, the second picks up where *Frankenstein Meets the Wolf Man*

left off. The two monsters are found frozen, and are thawed out yet again for another go at each other. By now the series is getting pretty thin, but if you love horror films you will still find plenty to like in this one.

SELECTED BIBLIOGRAPHY

Aylesworth, Thomas G. *Monsters from the Movies*. Philadelphia: Lippincott, 1972.

Baring-Gould, Sabine. *The Book of Werewolves*. New York: Causeway Books, 1973.

Boucher, Anthony. *The Compleat Werewolf*. New York: Simon & Schuster, 1969.

Cohen, Daniel. *A Natural History of Unnatural Things*. New York: Dutton, 1971.

————*Voodoo, Devils, and the New Invisible World*. New York: Dodd, Mead, 1972.

Douglas, Drake. *Horrors*. London: John Baler, 1987. Paper, Overlook Press, 1991.

Farson, Daniel. *Vampires, Zombies and Monster Men*. New York: Doubleday, 1976.

Garden, Nancy. *Werewolves*. Philadelphia: Lippincott, 1973.

Hamel, Frank. *Human Animals*. New Hyde Park, N.Y.: University Books, 1969.

Hill, Douglas and Pat Williams. *The Supernatural*. New York: Hawthorne, 1966.

Kriss, Marika. *Werewolves, Shapeshifters and Skinwalkers*. Los Angeles: Shelbourne Press, 1972.

McHargue, Georgess. *Meet the Werewolf*. Philadelphia: Lippincott, 1976.

O'Donnell, Elliott. *Werewolves*. New York: Longvue Press, 1965.

Otten, Charlotte F. (ed), A *Lycanthropy Reader*. Syracuse, N.Y.: Syracuse University Press, 1986.

Polley, Jane (ed). *American Folklore and Legend*. Pleasantville, N.Y.: The Readers Digest, 1978.

Pronzi, Bill (ed), *Werewolf!*. New York: Arbor House, 1979.

Reynolds, G.W.M. *Wagner the Wehr-Wolf*. New York: Dover, 1975.

Robbins, Rossell Hope. *The Encyclopedia of Witchcraft and Demonology*. New York: Crown, 1959.

Seabrook, William. *Witchcraft*. New York: Harcourt, Brace, 1940.

Stableford, Brian. *The Werewolves of London*. New York: Carroll & Graf, 1992.

Summers, Montague. *The Werewolf*. New Hyde Park, N.Y.: University Books, 1966.

Time-Life Books (ed). *Tales of Terror*, Alexandria, Va.: Time Life Books, 1987.

—— *Transformations*. Alexandria, Va.: Time-Life Books, 1989.

Van Doren Stern, Philip (ed). *Strange Beasts and Unnatural Monsters*. New York: Fawcett World Library, 1968.

Woodward, Ian. *The Werewolf Delusion*. New York: Paddington Press, 1979.